# Hit or Miss

# Hit or Miss

## Jeff Markowitz

E. L. Marker
Salt Lake City

E. L. Marker, an imprint of WiDō Publishing
Salt Lake City, Utah
widopublishing.com

Cover design by Steven Novak
Book design by Marny K. Parkin

ISBN 978-1-947966-48-2

**To Carol, now and always**

1

**Friday, May 8, 1970**

"WE HAVE A RESPONSIBILITY TO END THE WAR," EMILY insisted. "Otherwise, they died for nothing."

On Monday, the National Guard had shot and killed four students at Kent State University. Within days, there was talk of a massive demonstration to be held in Washington, DC. Emily was determined to be there.

She smiled innocently at Ben. "You don't want them to have died for nothing, do you?"

"Of course not."

"Then you'll go with me?"

"I don't know."

"Is it the baseball game?" She knew that Ben and his father went to the ballpark whenever the Giants were in town. "Surely ending the war is more important than a baseball game."

Emily could tell from the expression on Ben's face that he didn't have an answer. He sighed and scratched the corner of his eyebrow.

"Explain to me again what we'll be doing."

"We'll be ending the war."

"Okay," he said. "Ending the war is a good thing, but that's not what I mean. When we get to DC, what are we going to do?

Where are we going to sleep?"

Emily had it all figured out. "We'll head for the White House."

"I don't think President Nixon is going to put us up for the night."

Emily smacked his arm. "Don't be silly. We can spend the night on the street."

"I don't think I can do that."

"So, you'd rather go to a baseball game with your father than join me at the demonstration?"

"I don't know." Ben stared at the ground. "I don't know."

"It's time you stood up to your father." Emily bit her lip, worried this had hit harder than she intended. It couldn't be easy for Ben to embrace civil disobedience when his father was a cop. "Can you at least tell him you're not a Giants fan?"

On Friday, Emily rode a Greyhound bus, alone, to Washington, DC.

Greyhound had put on extra buses to DC as kids dressed in bell bottom jeans and dashikis jammed the terminal. It was the first indication that the demonstration in Washington was going to be large. As the bus sped through the night, Emily worried about the distance growing between her and Ben.

The bus made good time, rolling through Delaware and Maryland before arriving at last at its final destination: Union Station, Washington, DC.

A black man approached her in the station. She pegged him as in his late twenties, with an enormous Afro. He wore a brown leather jacket with fringe on the sleeves.

"Are you okay?"

"Me?" Emily looked around nervously. There weren't a lot of black men in the suburbs where she grew up. "Yes, I'm fine."

"You just got off the New York bus. My girlfriend recognized you."

Emily refrained from telling the man that he was mistaken, but there was no way this man's girlfriend knew her.

The man smiled warmly. "She's in the ladies' room. She told me not to let you out of my sight."

Emily turned and looked toward the ladies' room. A young brown-skinned woman with a close-cropped Afro exited the restroom. Before Emily could say anything, the woman walked off without acknowledging either of them.

A second woman stepped out of the restroom. She was fair-skinned with freckles on her cheeks and sizzling red hair that filled the space around her like a Rube Goldberg contraption. Dressed in faded bell bottoms and a tie-dyed T-shirt, her history professor, Miss Cooper, approached. She wore an ankle bracelet adorned with tiny bells that tinkled as she walked. Her professor was tinkling in Union Station.

"Do you have a place to stay tonight, Emily?"

She stared at Miss Cooper's ankle. "I'll figure something out."

"You can crash at our place." Miss Cooper smiled. "On Monday, I'll go back to being Miss Cooper, but for now, you can call me Willow."

Emily tried it out. "Willow." It felt funny in her mouth.

"My friend here—my old man—you can call him Bug."

Bug executed an elaborate bow from the waist.

Willow laughed. "Bug is a writer."

"A writer . . . wow, that's great. Have I read anything of yours?"

Willow answered for him. "Not yet, but he's almost finished

with an amazing manuscript."

Bug interrupted her. "One day I'll be a famous author. Until then, I wash dishes at the ashram."

"A writer and a dishwasher. Now I'm impressed." Emily giggled. "What's the book about?"

Bug grew serious. "Nirvana. Satori. The nature of enlightenment."

"That's awesome. I'd like to read it sometime."

Bug rooted through his knapsack, looking for his notebook. Willow stopped him. "You can do that later."

Bug nodded. "Let's head for the apartment. We'll need a good night's sleep if we're going to end the war tomorrow."

They took a cab to an apartment building on C Street SW. The building was a four-story walk-up. Their destination was on the fourth floor.

Bug jiggled the key in the lock until the door popped open. It was a simple, no-frills apartment, clean and functional. There was a sitting room with a futon, an alcove with a desk and bookcase, a small eat-in kitchen, a bathroom, and a bedroom in the back.

Emily fell asleep on the futon reading Bug's manifesto on the nature of enlightenment.

A knock on the door aroused her. Shaking the sleep from her body, Emily opened the door to a gaggle of hippies.

"Bug?" one asked, and they swooped into the apartment with their backpacks and bedrolls, their guitars and their blues harps, bandanas, sandals, mandalas, and marijuana. They sat down in a circle on the floor. Someone rolled a joint.

Willow came out to join them. "Hey, cool. Everybody, this is Emily, but you can call her Moonbeam. Moonbeam, these are my friends." She rattled off the names. "Rainbow, Dharma,

Patchouli, Stoner, Seymour, and Lily."

Willow gave Lily a hug. "He's in the bedroom."

Willow took Lily's place in the circle. Lily took Willow's place in the bedroom. Moonbeam watched them from a safe distance in the alcove.

No one got much sleep. They got high. They chanted. They finished off a box of Sugar Smacks. By morning, they were ready to end the war.

DETECTIVE MILLER GREW UP A FAN OF THE NY BASEBALL Giants. When the team moved to San Francisco, he had a few choice words for their owner, but he remained faithful to the club. He would take Ben to Mets games, but only when the Giants were in town.

They got to the ballpark in time to watch batting practice; but first, they stopped to watch the pitchers warm up. At Shea, the bullpen was separated from the parking lot by a simple chain link fence. Before going inside, they made it a habit to stop along the fence and chat with the pitchers and catchers.

Ben didn't have the heart to tell his father he wasn't a fan of the team from San Francisco. So, he cheered loudly for the Giants, for Willie Mays and Willie McCovey; but he rooted silently for the Mets, for Bud Harrelson and Ed Kranepool and especially for the pitchers, Tom Seaver, Jerry Koosman, and Nolan Ryan.

They ordered hot dogs from the hot dog vendor and peanuts from the peanut vendor. Detective Miller bought two beers and drank them both himself. Ben tried to buy a Rheingold, but his father cancelled the order.

"I don't like it when you drink."

"That's not fair." Ben stared at his father. "I'm not a kid anymore."

"You're still my kid." Detective Miller grinned.

"That's stupid."

"It's the law."

"No, it's not." Ben glared at his father. "You, of all people, should know that."

"Well, it's my law."

The Giants won the game 7-1. Ben decided it was the wrong time to tell his father he was a Mets fan.

They argued in the car on the drive home from Shea.

Detective Miller scanned the familiar streets in their neighborhood. Several streetlights had burned out. "Your girlfriend lives in one of these houses?"

"That one." Ben pointed to the white split-level. The front door was wide open. "Something's wrong."

Detective Miller pulled his car to the curb. "Wait here."

Tables and chairs had been overturned. The house was quiet.

Detective Miller called out for the Bayards, but there was no answer. He ran upstairs. The detective called out again. The door to the master bedroom was wide open. Dresser drawers were open. Random items of clothing were strewn about the room.

Ben followed his father into the bedroom.

"I told you to wait in the car."

Ben ignored his father. He checked on Duncan Bayard, who lay motionless on his side of the bed.

"His breathing is shallow." Ben shook him, but he was unresponsive. "What about Mrs. Bayard?"

Detective Miller didn't answer. Mrs. Bayard was suspended, her legs still in bed, tangled up in the blanket. Her torso dangled over the side of the bed, her head just a few inches off the floor.

"Is she . . . ?"

The detective shook his head. Mrs. Bayard was dead, the victim of a burglary gone bad.

Detective Miller placed a call to the station. The EMTs were quick to arrive on the scene. Two uniformed officers followed close behind. The officers secured the property. The EMTs rushed upstairs.

"Hey, Detective. Give us a hand getting him down the stairs."

As they made their way carefully down the stairs, the EMTs briefed the detective. They were taking Duncan Bayard to Franklin General. Mrs. Bayard was DOA. They would see to her transport later.

When the ambulance pulled away, Detective Miller went to his car and retrieved a Polaroid camera. He took a photo of the front door and made a note in his notepad. *No sign of forced entry.* He took a few photos of the overturned furniture and scribbled in the notepad. *Burglary?* Upstairs, he took dozens of Polaroids. The open dresser drawers. The clothes strewn across the room. The carpet. Mrs. Bayard, dead, half in and half out of her bed. A close-up of the red marks around her mouth and nose. In his notepad, he drew a diagram of the bedroom. He turned to Ben.

"Where's Emily?"

THOUSANDS OF YOUNG PEOPLE WERE ON THE MALL, AND more streamed in by the minute. Willow and her hippie friends staked out a spot near the Lincoln Memorial. Emily wandered the length of the National Mall, from the Lincoln Memorial to the Capitol Building and back again, determined to take it all in.

There was a buzz in the morning air. The President appeared unannounced on the Ellipse at dawn and chatted with a small group of demonstrators. He wished them an enjoyable stay in the nation's capital. Everyone Emily met on the Mall claimed to have seen him. The day was hot; the Mall was dry and dusty. There were crowds of people everywhere, an uneasy mixture of anti-war protestors, soldiers and police units, newsmen and onlook-ers. Protestors flashed peace signs and sang the fish cheer. Young Republicans responded with middle-finger salutes.

Emily didn't know most of the speakers at the demonstration, but she liked the message. End the Cambodian incursion. End the war in Vietnam. She located a payphone and used her spare change to call Ben.

"It's amazing. You should be here." She had to yell to be heard. Demonstrators continued to pour into the Mall. "Is anything happening in Dutch Neck?"

"You need to come home."

"Don't be like that."

"That's not what I mean. It's your mother."

"What about my mother?"

Ben didn't answer right away. The phone line crackled with static.

A scuffle broke out on the Mall. Police moved in quickly, weapons at the ready, cutting the small group of protestors off from the larger crowd. The confrontation pulled Emily's attention away from the phone call.

"Emily. Emily! Your mother is dead."

Later, the news would report that there were more than one hundred thousand demonstrators on the National Mall, but at that moment, amidst the pushing and shoving, Emily felt alone in the world.

Without more change to feed the phone, the line went dead. She dropped the payphone and turned, nearly bumping into a cop.

"Stay back," he ordered, his hand on his weapon.

"She's dead," she replied and kept walking.

He pointed the gun at Emily's head. "Who's dead?"

She could feel anger in the policeman, but also restraint. Days removed from Kent State, it was as if no one wanted to provoke the next shooting. The policeman holstered his weapon. Shouts of "pig" were replaced by prayers for peace. Emily breathed a sigh of relief and answered the officer's question.

"My mother."

"Do you have a way to get home?"

Emily told the officer about Miss Cooper and the apartment on C Street. He offered to give her a ride. If anyone saw her in the patrol car, she would tell them that she had been arrested.

No one answered when she knocked on the apartment door. The apartment manager was polite, but firm. She would have to leave.

"Do you need money for a bus ticket?" The officer reached for his wallet. "I'll drop you off at the bus station."

When Emily left Dutch Neck, her mother had been alive. If she got on a bus, she would be admitting that her mother was dead. She wasn't prepared to deal with that. Not yet. So, she decided to spend another night in DC. As long as she remained in DC, she told herself, she could pretend nothing was wrong at home. And maybe, just maybe, she could help end the war.

With no place else to go, she retraced her steps.

The crowd at the National Mall was smaller. There was a chill in the air, the midday heat a distant memory. It was a tough night, out on the Mall, trying not to think about her mother. Instead she thought about the American boys who were spending the night in rice paddies on the other side of the world, probably trying not to think about their mothers, too, and she knew that this was a small price to pay to end the war.

At four in the morning, an older man approached. He was dressed like an off-duty policeman heading out to play a round of golf.

"Are you here to end the war, miss?"

"Yes, I guess I am." She took a closer look at the middle-aged man and jumped to her feet. "Mr. President?"

President Nixon chuckled quietly.

"But, what . . . ?"

"I couldn't sleep. I thought some fresh air would do me good."

"But—"

"You know, sometimes I think you young people actually believe that I like being at war."

Emily didn't know how to answer the Commander in Chief. "Begging your pardon, sir, but it does sometimes seem that way."

"Let me tell you something, miss—by the way, we haven't been properly introduced. My name is Richard Nixon. And yours is?"

"Emily Bayard." She started to raise her fist in protest, like Bug did at the demonstration, but she couldn't extend her arm, not while she stood face-to-face with the President. She looked around, grateful that Willow and her friends weren't there to see her pitiful attempt at protest.

"Well, Emily, let me tell you something. I think I hate this war more than you do. But sometimes war is the necessary thing to do."

"But you could end the war, sir. You could end the war today."

"General Westmoreland tells me we need two more years to achieve our goals. You wouldn't want us to leave now, without achieving our goals. Give me two more years, Emily, and I'll end the war. You have my word on it."

"I don't think I can do that, sir."

President Nixon shook his head in sadness. "You young people can be so impatient."

"In a few weeks, I'll graduate from college."

"Congratulations. And then?"

"I don't know. But I have classmates . . . friends . . . they've been called up. In two years' time, they could be dead."

President Nixon didn't have an answer at the ready. "I'd best be on my way." The sun peeked over the horizon. "Before my Secret Service detail realizes I've slipped out."

President Nixon turned to leave. He took a few steps and then turned back to face Emily. "I've just had an idea. Are you hungry? Would you like to have breakfast with me?"

"You mean, like, in the White House?"

The President grinned. "I have the best chef. What would you like? You can have anything, anything at all. After all, I am the President."

"This isn't some sort of photo op, is it? You know what I mean, *antiwar activist sees the error of her ways after breaking bread with the President.*"

"I see what you mean. It would sure look good in the papers. Lord knows I could use a good story in the papers." The President chuckled. "No. No photos. No press release. You have my word."

And so it came to pass, on Sunday morning, before taking a bus back to Long Island to bury her mother, Emily had breakfast with the President. Mr. Nixon had poached eggs and corned beef hash with a cup of coffee, black. Emily had blueberry blintzes and a cup of chamomile tea. And all the while, they argued about the war.

"Would you like seconds?"

But she had put it off long enough. "I'm needed at home."

BEN WAS WAITING FOR HER WHEN EMILY CLIMBED OFF THE bus.

"Friday night, on our way home from the ballgame . . . your front door was wide open . . . your mother . . ."

Ben stared through the windshield at the traffic on Franklin Avenue. He didn't dare look at Emily in the passenger's seat, crying.

"What about my father?"

"Your father is in the hospital."

When they got to Franklin General, a doctor was examining Duncan Bayard. Emily tried to push her way in, but a nurse blocked her way.

"Please take a seat," she insisted. "I promise I'll come get you as soon as the doctor is finished."

The seats in the waiting room were molded plastic, bolted to the floor and remarkably uncomfortable. Ben did his best to distract Emily while they waited.

"Do you know why you can't hear a pterodactyl go to the bathroom?" It was Ben's favorite joke.

"I don't know. Why can't you hear a pterodactyl urinate?"

"Because the $p$ is silent." Ben laughed at his own joke. He was grateful that Emily did as well. He wanted to tell her another joke.

The dumber the better. But that was the only joke he could remember.

"Would you like to read a copy of my speech?" Commencement was only weeks away.

"I didn't think you wanted me to see it."

"I didn't." Ben knew Emily wanted him to speak out against the war. He didn't think he could do that, but he didn't want to disappoint her. Ben pushed that problem down the road.

He was spared, for the moment, by a candy striper with a message for Emily.

"You can see him now."

"I'll wait here," Ben said.

"No, you won't." Emily grabbed his hand and pulled him to his feet. "You're coming with me."

They didn't know what to expect, but when they entered his room, Duncan Bayard sat up in bed, connected to multiple machines. His face was ashen, his hair limp, his chest sunken in, but he was alive and conscious. Under the circumstances, Ben thought that was pretty good.

Emily stared at the tubes connected to her father. "How are you?"

He smiled weakly. "Come here."

She wrapped herself in her father's arms.

"Be careful about your dad's IV."

At the sound of Ben's voice, Emily's father groaned. Ben edged toward the door. He knew that Emily's father didn't like him. Duncan Bayard had told him that on more than one occasion.

"How are you feeling, Dr. Bayard?" Duncan Bayard was a PhD chemist, but he liked to be called doctor. For Emily's sake, Ben obliged.

Dr. Bayard focused his attention on Emily as if she had been the one to ask.

"My throat hurts. Like it's been rubbed raw. My nose is sore. I'm exhausted. Otherwise, I guess I'm okay."

Emily nodded. "What did the doctor say?"

"He said he's waiting for the lab tests."

"Did he say anything else?"

Duncan Bayard didn't answer his daughter's question. Instead, he posed one of his own. "What about your mother? No one will tell me how she's doing."

Like a low-lying fog, an uncomfortable silence descended in the room. Ben snuck a look at Emily, wondering what she would say. Ben knew that Emily was not the kind of girl who could lie to her father. Even for his own good.

"Mom's dead."

Dr. Bayard slumped down in the bed. "I'm tired," he said, closing his eyes.

The rest of the day, while her father slept, Emily sat by his side. When he wasn't sleeping, he complained about his throat. Emily offered him ice chips, but they didn't seem to help. He hurt in ways that ice chips couldn't soothe. Emily projected a brave front, sitting at her father's side, touching his arm, smoothing his bedclothes, but Ben could tell that Emily was hurting, too.

WHEN DETECTIVE MILLER GOT TO THE HOSPITAL, Dr. Bayard was shuffling down the hallway, dragging an IV pole, his ass peeking out of the hospital gown.

"Hey, it's great to see you up and about. I take it you're feeling better."

Duncan was slow to respond. Detective Miller figured that was a result of the medication and gave him all the time he needed. Eventually, Duncan replied.

"Just following doctor's orders. Taking my morning constitutional."

"Glad to know you're feeling better. What do the doctors say?"

"You know how it is. They say plenty, but not so as you can understand any of it."

For a moment, the detective was puzzled. "Oh, that's right. I forget sometimes you're not a real doctor."

Duncan Bayard bristled. He stood up as straight as possible, holding the IV pole with one hand and his hospital gown with the other. "I'll have you know that I have a PhD in chemistry."

"I'm sorry. I meant to say, you're not a medical doctor. No offense intended."

"None taken." Dr. Bayard paused. "What can you tell me about my wife?"

"Nothing yet. I'll know more when I get the autopsy report."

The two men walked in silence the rest of the way back to Dr. Bayard's room. In the privacy of the room, Detective Miller had a few more questions.

"What do you remember about Friday night? Can you tell me anything about your assailant?"

"I'm sorry, Detective, but I don't remember anything. That is to say, I remember going to bed in my house and waking up here in the hospital."

"Nothing about the assailant? What he looked like? What he said? Anything?"

"I'm sorry, no."

"Okay, then. Let's back up a bit. What did you and Mrs. Bayard do Friday evening?"

"I was at my office. Mrs. Bayard, I assume, was watching television."

Dr. Bayard sat down in the chair by his hospital bed. Detective Miller slumped down to avoid towering over him.

"Do you normally work so late on a Friday night?"

"I'm heading up an important project. We're behind schedule. I stayed at the office to get caught up."

"I've always been curious what a chemist does, exactly. If you don't mind my asking, what kind of project are you working on?"

"Deforestation." Dr. Bayard straightened up in the chair. "It's top secret. If I told you any more, I'd have to kill you."

"We don't want that. Anyway, you were at the office. Were you alone?"

"Of course. Except for my secretary, I was all alone. It wouldn't be fair to ask the team members to stay late on a Friday. Anyway, I was mostly reading reports."

"And when you finished at the office?"

"I went straight home. It was about eleven. I remember because Mrs. Bayard was already in bed, watching the evening news."

"So, everything at home was normal?" The detective checked his notes. "Tables and chairs had been knocked over. It was obvious your home had been ransacked."

"I can assure you, Detective, nothing was out of the ordinary. When the news ended, I turned off the TV and fell asleep. I assume Mrs. Bayard did the same. The next thing I remember, I was in the emergency room."

"I am sorry for your loss."

"One last thing, Detective." His throat was sore, his voice raspy. "Catch the SOB who murdered my wife."

"I will. You have my word on it."

# 6

DETECTIVE MILLER CALLED THE MEDICAL EXAMINER'S office and asked about the autopsy. He listened to the shuffling of papers at the other end of the phone line.

"I'm sorry, Detective, that autopsy hasn't been completed yet."

"When do you expect to have it finished?"

"Let me check on that." The clerk put him on hold and returned after a long minute. "The case hasn't been assigned yet."

"What's that mean, not assigned yet? I'm the lead detective. It's assigned to me."

"I'm sorry. When I said not assigned, I was referring to which one of our doctors would be doing the autopsy."

"Look, I know you don't make the assignments, but—"

"That's right. I don't make the assignments."

"It's just, there's a young lady. Her father is in the hospital. Her mother is in the morgue. I'd like to be able to tell her something."

One more time, the detective could hear the shuffling of papers on the other end of the phone line. "Can you come to the medical examiner's office tomorrow?"

The medical examiner's office was located at Meadowbrook Hospital, in East Meadow, about a thirty-minute drive from Dutch

Neck. The old hospital had been there since 1935. The coroner's unit was a more recent addition. Rather than assign the autopsy to one of his staff, Dr. Morello, Chief Medical Examiner for the county, agreed to expedite the case.

The two men stood in the morgue, looking at the body of Mrs. Rosalie Bayard. Detective Miller found it difficult to stay focused. It wasn't so much the dead body that was the source of the distraction. It was the wall of drawers. It was the bodies he couldn't see that distracted the detective.

Dr. Morello showed him how her blood had darkened and formed clumps in blood vessels and in bodily organs. He showed him how her mucous membranes were red and inflamed. He talked about the tell-tale signs of chloroform. He pointed to the red scoring around her lips.

"It's easy to recognize, as long as you know what to look for. Fifty years ago, doctors were familiar with chloroform. Today, not so much. But the lab test is simple. It's not so very different than it was at the turn of the century, when chemists were taught to chop up a tissue sample, boil it, treat it chemically, and watch for its signature color change."

The detective didn't give a fig about the science. He just wanted to know the result. "So, the cause of death was chloroform?"

"Cardiac arrest resulting from chloroform poisoning."

"When can I expect your report?"

"We're pretty busy. It could take a couple of weeks to generate the official report. That's why I suggested you come down here today."

"Thanks for your help, Doc. Can I buy you a cup of coffee? I could use a crash course in chloroform."

"We can get a cup of coffee in the cafeteria. It's positively horrid stuff." Dr. Morello chuckled.

"It's got to be better than the stuff that passes for coffee at the station house."

They walked through the hallway and down one flight of stairs to the hospital cafeteria. Dr. Morello spotted a colleague sitting at an otherwise empty table. He introduced the detective to Dr. Daniel Rosenberg, anesthesiologist.

"This is Detective Miller. He needs to know about chloroform."

"For a case, I assume?"

The detective nodded. "Rosalie Bayard."

"Chloroform was a popular form of anesthesia used in surgeries from 1850 until approximately 1920. It was also used as an ingredient in a variety of medical potions. But by 1940, it ceased to be used for any legitimate medical purposes."

"How come?"

"People died. Not as many as you might think, but enough to cause concern. And by 1940, anesthesiologists had better, safer alternatives. Is that what killed Mrs. Bayard?"

Dr. Morello had been sipping his coffee while Dr. Rosenberg briefed the detective. "I found cardiac arrest as a result of chloroform poisoning."

Detective Miller checked his notes. "Mrs. Bayard died when a burglar used chloroform to knock her out. How much would it take?"

"Probably just an ounce or two. Soak a handkerchief, hold it over her face for a couple of minutes."

"So, the question is, where would the burglar get his hands on a couple of ounces of chloroform? I mean, it's not the sort of thing you can just walk into a pharmacy and buy, is it?"

"No, of course not."

"Does the hospital have a supply?"

"Like I said, there has been no legitimate medical use of chloroform for at least thirty years."

"Would you know if there are any legitimate non-medical uses for chloroform?"

Dr. Rosenberg thought for a moment before responding. "Manufacturing. Of course, I'm no expert," he added quickly, "but I think chloroform can be used as a refrigerant."

"Refrigerant?"

"You know . . . air conditioners."

"Thank you, Doctor." Detective Miller scribbled in his notepad. "Do you know where I could find an expert?"

"I imagine your best bet would be to talk to someone in the chemical industry. I'm afraid I can't help you with a name."

Detective Miller made another note in his notepad. "That's quite all right. I may know someone."

## 7

DETECTIVE MILLER WAS PLEASED TO LEARN THAT Dr. Bayard had been discharged and was recuperating at home. He knocked at the Bayards' front door.

Emily opened the door. Before he had a chance to step inside, she bombarded the detective with questions. "Have you spoken to the medical examiner? Do you know how my mother died?"

"Yes and yes." Detective Miller edged into the house and turned to face Dr. Bayard, who sat on a couch in the living room. "How are you feeling?"

"Physically, I'm doing pretty well. Emotionally, I'm sure you can understand."

Emily refilled her father's water glass. "Can I get you something to drink, Detective?"

"No, thank you."

"Do you have news about my mother?"

Detective Miller checked his notes while considering how much to say. "The cause of death was cardiac arrest as a result of chloroform poisoning. We are still in the preliminary stages of the investigation, but my working theory is that the burglars used chloroform to knock out your parents before ransacking the house."

Dr. Bayard did his best to keep up with the conversation. "But we were both chloroformed."

Detective Miller repeated what he had been told at the morgue. "People can have very different reactions to chloroform."

"Do you have any leads?"

"Like I said, it's still early in the investigation. Now that we know about the chloroform, that's where I'm starting. Perhaps there have been other burglaries where the homeowners were knocked out. Maybe we can identify where the burglars got their hands on the chloroform. That's why I'm here. I hope you can be helpful with that."

"If it will help you find the man who murdered my wife . . . just tell me what I can do."

"You're a chemist."

"Yes, I am."

"I understand that chloroform has no valid medical uses anymore. I never was any good at science, but I imagine the chemical industry must use chloroform for something."

"Chloroform is used to make refrigerants."

"Refrigerants?"

"Yes. For air conditioning. Also, nonstick cookware. Have you ever heard of Teflon?"

"I don't think so." Detective Miller took out his notepad and wrote *Teflon*.

"You will, soon enough. Of course, that's not my area of expertise."

"That's right, you told me." The detective checked his notes. "Something to do with trees."

Dr. Bayard lapsed into silence. It was time for the detective to take his leave.

"Again, I am sorry for your loss."

8

BEN STOOD THERE FEELING AWKWARD, SHIFTING HIS WEIGHT clumsily from one foot to the other while Emily said goodbye to her mother. The funeral home began to fill up. Ben stood next to Emily, the dutiful boyfriend, as she greeted those in attendance.

Mrs. Bayard was dressed in a simple green dress and a single strand of pearls. The funeral home had applied just enough make-up to hide the red marks on her face. Emily took one look at her mother and grabbed Ben for support.

"Mom always told me, when I got married, she'd give them to me. But I could never wear them now. And it will bring my father some measure of comfort, knowing that they remain around her neck."

Ben's parents made a brief appearance to pay their last respects. His father stopped to sign the guest book, but Ben could tell he was using the opportunity to match names and faces. The detective, always on the job.

The Roman Catholic Church was a large white plaster building with a row of stained-glass windows lining one wall. Rosalie Bayard had been a popular member of the community, active in the PTA, a regular at bridge and mah jongg. The church was crowded.

The priest called on Emily's Aunt Debbie to read a passage. Then it was Emily's turn. She spoke quietly.

"'Death is nothing at all. It does not count. I have only slipped away into the next room.'"

She managed to get through the passage without shedding tears. In the pew, Ben cried enough for the both of them.

After mass, they made the long slow drive to the cemetery and then home. The neighbors had set up a buffet table with baked ziti, cold cuts, and salads. The house wasn't as crowded as the church, but it was far from empty.

Emily squeezed through a crowd of neighbors and their heartfelt condolences. A middle-aged man in a brown suit and tie blocked her passage. Tortoise-shell glasses sat crookedly on his aquiline nose. His hair smelled like brylcreem. It took Emily a moment to recognize Mr. Gillis from her father's chem lab.

"I like what you said at the church."

"Thank you."

"I'm sure this has been hard on you."

A woman in a well-tailored suit and blouse joined the conversation. "It's been hard on all of us."

Something about the woman made Emily uncomfortable. *Don't trust anyone over thirty.* Then she took a closer look. The woman was only a few years older than Emily, still on the younger side of the generational divide. Somehow, that didn't make Emily feel any better.

"I'm Karen Conaway. I work with your father." She reached for Emily's hand. "I'm sorry."

Across the room, Emily made eye contact with Ben. *Get me out of here.*

"There you are," he said, sprinting across the room. "I've been looking for you."

Karen Conaway smiled. "I'm sorry for your loss."

# 9

BEN STOOD AT THE PODIUM AND LOOKED OUT AT THE SEA of folding chairs on the dead and dying grass that was the college campus. Richardson College was a commuter school composed of four identical buildings, arranged to form a quad housing the administration, departmental offices, classrooms, and student union, surrounded by parking lots. Ben had wanted to go to a big school in California, but his parents couldn't afford it. Emily's father was on the Board of Trustees at Richardson. So, he ended up at Richardson, a school so close to home, most days he commuted on foot.

There was, of course, one thing Richardson had that no West Coast college could offer . . . Emily.

The sun peeked out behind the chairs, glowing orange. To his back, the moon was pale white, low in the sky and unsettled. He pulled the speech from his pocket, carefully unfolding the papers. The empty chairs ignored him as he practiced.

*It's a good speech*, he told himself, *a perfectly acceptable speech suitable for the occasion*. Ben was aiming for insightful, but not too insightful. Funny, but not too funny. His friends would probably call it boring, but not too boring.

It was, in a word, moderate. No one would be surprised by that. He was, after all, moderate in his beliefs and in his behavior.

But Emily had been pushing him to speak out publicly against the war.

Ben folded the paper and shoved it back in his pocket. He had worked on the speech for weeks. He was running out of time.

He hurried home, letting himself in through the screen door on the side of the house. His mother was in the kitchen, preparing breakfast for the two men in her life. She poured him a glass of orange juice and smiled.

"Good morning, dear. You're up early. Is everything okay?"

"I'm fine." *How much should I tell her?* "I'm thinking about re-writing the speech."

"Your father told me your speech is perfect. It's normal if you're feeling nervous."

"It's not nerves."

"Then what is it?" She checked his forehead. "You're not running a fever."

"It's supposed to be my speech, isn't it?"

"It is your speech."

"No, it's not. Not really." He wanted her to understand but didn't know where to begin.

"Your father—"

He didn't let her finish. "That's what I'm trying to tell you. Of course Dad likes the speech; he wrote most of it."

"He's very proud of you. I am, too. He just wants the day to be perfect for you."

"He wants the day to be perfect for him."

"You'll feel better after you have your breakfast." She kissed him on the forehead. "I know you'll do the right thing."

Ben had spent a lifetime doing the right thing. Why would she expect anything else? And, he told himself, he still wanted to do the right thing, but it was getting harder with every passing day to know what the right thing was.

He opened his desk and removed a small gift box, a graduation present from Emily. Hippie dog tags, she called them. *War is not healthy for children and other living things.* He slipped them on under his shirt. Ben liked the way they felt, cold against his chest.

By the time they got to Richardson, the parking lots were filled to capacity. Ben hopped out, leaving his parents to find a parking place. Two hours until commencement, but school was bedlam. He made his way through the clogged hallway, heading for the student union to pick up his cap and gown. And, he hoped, where he'd find Emily. Since her mom's death, Emily had lost interest in graduation.

He spotted her across the crowded room, talking to their history professor. Miss Cooper was tall and thin, her red hair barely contained under a yellow knitted cap. Emily was shorter, just the right height for kissing if she stood on her tiptoes, with long blonde hair that she ironed every night. Emily talked with her hands when she was excited. She would have made a fabulous signalman in the navy air corps, except, of course, for her politics and her gender. Ben watched, waiting for her to notice.

Suddenly, Emily squealed and pushed her way through the crowded room. She threw her arms around Ben and gave him a kiss. The perfect height. "Are you ready?"

At the center of a small knot of dignitaries, Emily's father, Dr. Bayard, held court. He was still weak and his throat sore, but he was vice-president of the Board of Trustees. He would not miss his daughter's graduation.

"It's a big day today, Benjamin."

"Yes, Dr. Bayard. That it is."

Dr. Bayard patted Ben on the back, warily, like a stray dog. "I'm looking forward to your speech. I trust you've written something suitably inspirational?"

"I hope so."

When it was Ben's turn to speak, he nearly missed his cue. He removed the perfectly acceptable speech from his pocket, unfolded the paper, and began to read.

"Dean Dalrymple, Dr. Bayard, distinguished guests, faculty, family members and friends, and especially fellow members of the class of 1970, Greetings.

"When we arrived at Richardson, we were fresh out of high school, mere children in a grown-up world. Were we ready for college? Probably not. And yet here we are. This is the very last time that we will all be together, and I am proud to stand before you today, proud to say that the class of 1970 . . ."

And then he stopped. He stood on the podium and said nothing. Ben heard nervous laughter from the audience. He put the speech back in his pocket and started over.

"No graduating class has a monopoly on matters of right or wrong, of good or evil. But we are the class of 1970, and the dangers we face are uniquely our own. After graduation, some of us will be on our way to Vietnam. We have a proud tradition of military service in this country . . . in this community . . . and in my own family . . . but it is hard to take pride in our military when we see the nightly news reports from Southeast Asia. It is hard to take pride in so much death and dying. To my friends who will soon find themselves buried up to their hips in mud and blood, I ask you only to serve with honor and to come home as soon as possible, safe and in one piece."

No one was laughing any more.

"Last year, in history, Miss Cooper taught us about the marketplace of competing ideas. It's a place where every idea is welcome. In that marketplace, we have a responsibility to examine ideas objectively, dispassionately. We have a responsibility to give as much attention to the ripeness of the ideas as we would in a 'real' market to our fruits and vegetables."

Ben looked out across the crowd and spotted Miss Cooper's red hair bouncing.

*How am I doing, Miss Cooper?*

From a space just below all that red hair, he heard her shout, "You're doing great, Benjamin."

"I've always believed that college is that kind of marketplace, filled with fabulous ideas just waiting for closer examination, Plato and Aristotle, Hegel and Nietzsche, J. D. Salinger.

"And then on May fourth, four college students were shot at Kent State University because our government didn't approve of their ideas."

He pushed ahead, ignoring the grumbles from the assembled audience.

"To my friends who have not yet completed their college studies, or who have plans to continue on to grad school, I ask you to study honorably and to come home safe and in one piece."

There was a moment of awkwardness when Ben walked across the stage to receive his diploma. His classmates received a diploma and a handshake. All Ben got was the diploma. Then Dr. Bayard approached the podium, offering a few congratulatory remarks to the class of 1970.

"I cannot, in good conscience, conclude this ceremony without reminding you of your duties and responsibilities to this great nation. As we sit here, America is at war. When America is at war, there can be no dissent. Dissent, such as we heard today, brings aid and comfort to the enemy.

"Where do our children get such foolish ideas? Certainly not at home from their parents. No. It pains me to say this, but apparently they find these treasonous ideas in some sort of illegal school store, operated by one of our professors—Miss Cooper, I believe—and I want to make a promise here, today, to all of the parents—the Board of Trustees will deal with Miss Cooper. We will shut down her marketplace. We will not allow Communist propaganda to infiltrate Richardson College."

At college commencement, Dr. Bayard accused Ben of giving aid and comfort to the enemy.

And then it was over. Everyone was jumping up and down, laughing and throwing their caps in the air. The graduating class of 1970. Ben wasn't sure what to do. He'd never been an antiwar activist before. He'd never been an enemy of the state.

Fatty B ran over and slapped him on the back.

"Awesome speech!" He grinned. "I can't believe your dad let you say that stuff."

Ben looked around before responding. "He didn't."

"Oh man." Fatty B laughed. "You stepped in it this time."

Ben spotted Miss Cooper and tried to apologize for dragging her into this, but she wouldn't hear of it.

"At the start of every semester, I stand in front of a new class of students, and I wonder whether any of them will understand what I'm trying to teach. I wonder whether any of them will get it. Do you know what I mean?"

Ben didn't trust himself to say more than he already had.

"You got it." Miss Cooper beamed. "Oh man," she repeated. "You got it!"

"But your job . . . Dr. Bayard said . . ."

"I can handle that blowhard." And then she kissed him. Not a polite peck on the cheek. Miss Cooper planted a big, fat wet one square on his mouth.

"Bu-bu-bu—" His face was as red as her hair.

"Now go do something fabulous."

They say you can spot a cop by his shoes (apparently Ben was already learning to think like an enemy of the state). That was especially true if the shoes were a size twelve, wide, and they belonged to your father. Ben spotted the thick-soled, dark black brogans approach.

Miss Cooper saw them as well. "How nice to see you, Detective. I was just complimenting Ben on his speech."

"I saw what you were just doing." He turned to Fatty B. "Congratulations, Henry."

"Thank you, sir."

Finally he turned to Ben. The sun slipped behind a storm cloud.

"Quite a day."

"Yes."

"You changed the speech."

Ben couldn't suppress a smile. "Yes."

"We'll talk about that when we get home. Are you ready to leave?"

Detective Miller had the habit of asking questions as a polite way of delivering instructions. Ben decided, for once, to ignore the implied instruction. Surely as an enemy of the state, he couldn't be expected to go home with his parents. "I'll catch a ride later with one of my Communist friends."

"That's not funny."

As if on cue, Emily appeared at Ben's side.

Detective Miller smiled. "Congratulations, Emily. What did you think of Ben's speech?"

"I thought it was amazing. What did you think, sir?"

"I think he's going to be in a lot of trouble when he gets home." With that, Detective Miller turned and walked off, his black brogans slapping the ground hard with each step. He didn't bother turning around when he added, "Don't be late. We have plans."

✌

Ben's family lived in a quiet, residential neighborhood, mostly ranch houses and split-levels, with their neat little yards and their two-car garage. Ben was nearly home when he heard the footsteps.

"Hey, look at that. It's him."

They sped up, closing the gap, all the while shouting greetings. "Commie. Pinko. Faggot."

Ben picked up his pace, but within one block they had caught him. "America," one of them opined, "love it or leave it." And then he hit Ben on the jaw.

Ben was outnumbered, but he fought back as best he could. Finally, he covered his head and absorbed the blows on his arms. His assailants quickly grew bored and ran off, cursing and laughing.

Ben did a quick inventory of his injuries. The first punch had left a nasty bruise. His head throbbed. Otherwise he was okay. There was no blood evidence. Ben hurried home, letting himself in the side door.

It took his mother mere seconds to hone in on the bruise. "What happened to you?" She called for Ben's father.

"What happened?"

"A couple of classmates took exception to my speech."

His mother examined the bruise and made a quick decision. "Take him to Dr. Spinner's office. On the way home, you can stop at the station and fill out a complaint. I'll call Dr. Bayard and cancel dinner."

"I don't need to see Dr. Spinner. And I'm not signing a complaint." Ben stood his ground. "I'm fine." He turned to face his father. "Tell her I'm fine."

"He's fine, dear." Detective Miller stared at his son. "Go clean yourself up. We don't want to keep your girlfriend waiting, now, do we?"

It hurt Ben to smile. He smiled anyway. "Thanks, Dad."

They drove to the restaurant in silence. Pulling into the parking lot, the detective cleared his throat. "I need to say something before we go inside."

"Really, dear. Now? We're going to a party. Can't it wait?"

"No, I don't think it can." He paused to gather his thoughts. "You understand I don't agree with anything you said today."

"Yes sir, I understand."

"And yet you went ahead and said it anyway, in front of everyone."

"Yes, I guess I did."

"You embarrassed me in front of the entire community. I won't have that."

"So, that's what I am to you—an embarrassment?"

"That's not what I said."

"That's exactly what you said."

It was hot inside the car. "Well, it's not what I meant." His father had to have the last word. "Now go inside and smile. We're celebrating."

Ben spotted Emily right away. She was sitting at a table in the back with her father and her Aunt Debbie. She looked across the room at Ben and smiled.

Dr. Bayard sat with arms crossed. A frown had taken residence on his face.

The rear wall was mirrored floor to ceiling, reflecting the room, extending it as far as the eye could see. The table repeated itself, and in each of the reflected images, Dr. Bayard's frown looked increasingly severe.

"Look, Debbie, it's the Millers. How nice of you to—"

But before he could finish, Aunt Debbie interrupted.

"Oh my. What happened to Ben?"

Ben's mom was the first to respond. "He was attacked on the way home."

Emily jumped up and rushed to his side. She reached out, gently touching the bruise on his cheek. "Are you okay?"

"I'm fine. Really. It looks worse than it is."

Emily whispered in his ear. "It makes you look like Marlon Brando."

Detective Miller turned to Dr. Bayard. "On his way home, Ben met up with a couple of guys who took exception to his speech."

Dr. Bayard nodded unsympathetically. He picked up a glass of water and took a long sip before responding. "I don't as a rule condone violence, but there is a lesson to be learned here." He turned to address Ben directly. "If you're going to insult this great country, there are going to be consequences. Patriotic Americans will not put up with you badmouthing the US of A."

"I don't think Ben was badmouthing the US of A." Aunt Debbie smiled at Ben. "I thought it was a fine speech."

Dr. Bayard nearly dropped his glass of water. "You thought it was a fine speech? Did you even listen?"

"I don't pay as much attention to politics as you do, dear. But as a woman, I don't think I'd be happy if I lost a child in Vietnam."

Mrs. Miller reached into her purse for a hankie. "Let's order, why don't we?"

Detective Miller signaled for a waitress. Things grew quiet at the table as they studied the menu.

Ben ordered the prime rib.

"Soup or salad?"

Salad at Sid's was an enormous wedge of iceberg lettuce, swimming in salad dressing.

"I'll have the salad." Ben looked at his Dad and smirked. "With Russian dressing."

## 10

BEN GOT A JOB AT A CALL CENTER IN HEMPSTEAD. HE hated punching a timecard. He hated reading from a script. He hated pretending he was doing the caller a favor, offering them great works of literature, bound in faux leatherette, for just $4.95 per month ("That's less than seventeen cents a day," he was supposed to say). Emily took a summer job selling soft-serve ice cream. To break up the monotony, Ben would call Emily at the ice cream store.

He would adopt a phony accent and ask to speak to Cookiepuss. No matter how many times he called, it never stopped being funny. To Ben, that was. Emily was not so easily amused. Neither, apparently, was Ben's boss. Ben promised not to do it again. The next time he called, he asked for Fudgy the Whale. Ben's career in telephone sales promised to be temporary as well.

When she wasn't dishing out soft-serve ice cream, Emily spent most of her free time at the ashram with Bug and Willow. Ben didn't understand.

"The ashram," he asked. "That's a Hindu temple, right?"

"Yeah, kind of. This one's more of a Hindu coffee house."

"I thought you said Bug was Buddhist."

"His writing is Buddhist. His dishwashing is Hindu. His family, I think, is Baptist. What difference does it make?"

"A big difference," Ben insisted, but he never could say why. "You should go with me."

When the small retail shops were abandoned downtown in favor of the new shopping mall, the ashram moved into a vacant storefront on Main Street. The ashram was part prayer hall and part coffee house. It served as a sort of unofficial meeting place for the poets and potheads, the philosophers and feminists, the deadheads and redheads, in short, for anyone who identified themselves as part of the counterculture. It took Emily a few days to convince Ben to meet her there after work. He spotted Miss Cooper as soon as he stepped inside.

"Miss Coo—" Emily poked Ben in the ribs. "Willow."

Willow grinned. "It's good to see you here, Ben." She turned toward the kitchen and called for Bug.

"So, you're the dude who caused all the trouble at commencement? Willow can't stop talking about you." Bug grinned. "If I didn't know better, I'd be jealous."

Ben blushed at the very idea.

"Can I get you something from the kitchen?"

Emily answered for the both of them. "Ben will have a brown rice knish. I'll have the lentil soup."

While they ate, Willow tried to tell Ben about the ashram, but he was distracted. Ben still thought of her as Miss Cooper, his history professor, but in the ashram, she was a hippie, and a braless hippie at that. Ben tried not to look, but Emily could see he was peeking.

"They're adorable, aren't they?"

"I don't know what you're talking about," Ben stammered, his face bright red.

"There's no reason to be embarrassed. The human body is natural." Willow stood up. "I'll be in the prayer hall."

When they finished eating, Ben and Emily joined Willow in the prayer hall. She wasn't alone. Emily ran over.

"Hey, Dharma, Lily. Hey, Seymour."

"Moonbeam!"

Ben was confused. "Who's Moonbeam?"

"I'm Moonbeam," Emily explained, and she did seem to be beaming. "I told you about DC." She looked over at Dharma, sitting cross-legged on a prayer rug. "What's up?"

"We're planning an antiwar protest on the Fourth of July."

Seymour glared at Ben. "Who's the dude with Moonbeam?"

"He's my old man," Emily explained.

"He's the one I told you about," added Willow, "the one who gave the speech at commencement."

Ben bristled at the reference to the speech, like for the rest of his life that was how he was going to be identified. *The one who gave the speech at commencement.*

Seymour wasn't satisfied. "His father is a pig."

Ben tensed up at the word. "My father—"

"It's okay." Lily examined Ben carefully. "You're Billy Miller's little brother, aren't you?"

Ben didn't bother answering.

Willow had heard enough. "I'll vouch for Ben. Let's get back to work."

They spent the next hour debating how best to mount a demonstration on the Fourth. Nothing was big enough to satisfy Bug.

"We need to do something dramatic," he insisted, "something that will get people's attention."

Bug had it all figured out. "We should levitate the Pentagon."

## 11

WILLOW LIVED IN AN APARTMENT UPSTAIRS FROM A LUN-
cheonette in the old part of Dutch Neck. The aroma of steaming
hot chicken soup greeted Ben and Emily at the door.

"Are you hungry?"

"It smells wonderful. Did you make it?"

"Don't be silly, Ben. It's from the luncheonette."

"Well, it still smells wonderful."

Bug came out from the bedroom. He started to say something
to Willow but stumbled over his words and sputtered to a stop.
"I need to leave."

"You'll die of heat in that turtleneck." Willow frowned. "I can't
go with you."

"I understand."

"Don't get into trouble tonight."

Bug pulled on his leather jacket and left without making any
promises.

Emily ate most of her soup and then fell asleep, her head
pressed against the formica table.

"When is the last time she had a good night's sleep?" Willow
managed to get Emily on her feet. "Ben, give me a hand here."
Together, they walked Emily into the bedroom.

The room was austere, and at the same time opulent. There were India print fabrics hanging from the walls. The room had a creamy, wood smell. A wisp of smoke rose from a stick of sandalwood incense on a corner table. Also on the table were unframed art posters—Degas, Kandinsky, Chagall, and Gauguin. Ben spotted a book about transcendental meditation on the night table. Another book about tantric yoga. A pack of Zig Zag rolling papers. Red fabric was draped over the table lamp. A dresser drawer was open, revealing a pile of purple panties. Emily kicked off her sandals and collapsed on the bed.

Willow took charge. "Emily can sleep here tonight. Wait in the kitchen. I'll be right out."

Ben sat at the kitchen table, his thoughts all a-jumble. His girlfriend's mother was dead. Emily herself was asleep in the next room, overcome with exhaustion and grief. But all Ben could think about were Willow's purple panties.

Willow joined him at the kitchen table. "She'll sleep until morning. Now what about you?"

"Can I ask you a question, Miss Cooper?"

"You can, but only if you call me Willow."

"I'll try." But the words didn't come easily.

"How old do you think I am?"

"I don't know. Teacher years are different than people years." Willow smiled. "I'm twenty-eight."

"I guess I never thought of you as a person, you know what I mean? And I surely never imagined your bedroom like that." His face reddened. "Not that I ever imagined your bedroom. I mean it would be wrong if . . . I don't mean wrong, exactly . . . you know what I mean . . ."

Willow burst out laughing. "It's okay, Ben. Really, I'm flattered. Only I think maybe you've learned enough about me for one night. It's time for you to go home."

"I'm sorry if I did something wrong, Miss Cooper . . . I mean, Willow."

She walked Ben to the door and gave him a kiss. She pressed her body ever so slightly against his. He could tell she wasn't wearing a bra. She could tell . . . well, she could just tell.

"You didn't do anything wrong." She pushed him out the door. "You should leave before you do."

## 12

DETECTIVE MILLER DIDN'T MAKE IT A HABIT TO FREQUENT the local VFW, but Vice President Agnew was scheduled to speak. He would hear the Vice President and also pick up some much-needed overtime.

Junior Officer Tommy Callahan greeted him at the door. Son of a hero cop who died in the line of duty, Tommy was a card-carrying member of the Young Republicans, a middle-aged man in the body of a twenty-year-old. Since the death of Tommy's father, the police department had pretty much adopted Tommy, letting him hang out at the station house, helping out where he could. He passed the police exam shortly before his eighteenth birthday. When he completed the required college credits, Tommy would be eligible for an appointment with the Nassau County police. Until then, he helped out at the precinct. "You've been asking about chloroform."

Detective Miller looked up in surprise. "Have you heard something?"

"Not here," Tommy said quickly. "Do you remember Sonny's?"

Detective Miller used to meet Tommy's father there for coffee. "The place on Rockaway Ave?"

"Yeah."

"Is Tuesday okay?"

"I'll be there."

There were a few hundred guests, waiting to get into the VFW hall, mostly middle-aged men, many of them World War Two veterans, some wearing their service hats and medals. Detective Miller paid particular attention to a young black man, wearing a turtleneck in the summer heat. There was no reason to believe he had any specific plans to disrupt the event. Still, it was obvious he didn't belong. Detective Miller wondered whether he was supposed to turn the man away, but the Vice President's people were eager to avoid an incident. They checked the man's ticket, asked him a few questions, and ushered him into the auditorium.

There was a buzz in the room. The Post Commander approached the podium. He took an index card out of his jacket pocket and tapped the microphone. It took a few extra taps, but the room grew quiet.

"I'm pleased to be able to welcome all of you tonight. I'd especially like to welcome those of you who are here for the first time. It is gratifying to see such a large turnout for this very special event. I hope you'll come back for future activities. Now I would ask you all to stand and join me in the Pledge of Allegiance."

After leading the room in the pledge, and making a few, brief Post announcements, the Commander cleared his throat.

"Tonight's guest speaker needs no introduction. A former member of the United States Army, a member of the Veterans of Foreign Wars, having served with honor in World War Two and again in Korea, the recipient of a bronze star, a man who understands all too well the responsibility to protect this great nation from enemies without and within, I give you the Vice President of the United States, Spiro T. Agnew."

The Vice President entered through a side door to tumultuous applause and joined the Post Commander at the podium.

"Thank you, Commander. It is a privilege to be here in Dutch Neck."

The Post Commander waved to the Post's semi-official historian and waited until a photo had been taken to commemorate the meeting. After posing for the photo, the Commander reluctantly took a seat in the front row.

Agnew looked out on the crowd. The Vice President was beaming.

"Fellow Patriots," he began. "The American way of life is under attack. It is under attack in Vietnam. It is under attack in Cambodia. It is under attack here in Dutch Neck. It is under attack by Communists abroad and by Communist sympathizers here at home. I don't need to tell you what will happen if we let loony lefties and pinko pipsqueaks undermine our American will."

The crowd erupted in spontaneous applause. The Vice President basked in the warmth in the room.

"Recently, those loony lefties have been protesting our troops' activity in Cambodia. I am pleased to be able to report that the Cambodian campaign has successfully disrupted numerous attacks by the cowardly Viet Cong on our brave American boys. But our job is not done yet. Does anyone want us to leave before the job is finished?"

Before the audience could answer the Vice President's rhetorical question, the room was suffused in the smell of rotten egg.

As the first whiff of rotten egg reached the podium, three Secret Service agents whisked the Vice President out a side door. The remainder of the federal detail stood guard at the exits. No one would enter or leave until the Secret Service was satisfied. The majority would need only a cursory review. Republican donors, decorated veterans, pillars of the community, the Secret Service didn't waste much time before clearing them from any involvement in what they were already calling *the rotten egg incident.*

One of the feds pulled Detective Miller aside. "I want to interrogate the Black Panther."

Detective Miller's eyes went instinctively to the young black man in the back of the room. *Was he really a Black Panther?* Detective Miller was on high alert.

The fed grabbed the young man by the arm. "Come with me."

"Get your hands off me."

"Don't be stupid, son."

"I'm not your son!"

"What's your name?" The agent had one hand resting casually on his gun.

The young man grinned. "Bug."

The fed scowled. "Your real name."

Bug spit the words out. "George Thomas Bugge."

"Okay, then." It was the agent's turn to grin. "What do you know about the stink bomb, Mr. Bugge?"

"Nothing."

"So, what were you doing when the stink bomb went off?"

"Minding my own business. Listening to the Vice President."

"You don't strike me as the sort of person who would be interested in what Mr. Agnew has to say. Unless, of course, you were intending some sort of civil disobedience." The agent stared hard at Bug. "You weren't planning some sort of demonstration here tonight, were you?"

"No. Like I said, I was sitting in my seat, listening to the Vice President when the stink bomb went off."

"Who were you sitting with?"

"I'm here all by myself."

"By yourself? That seems odd."

"I'm not responsible for how things seem to you."

"Okay then, let's try this one more time. What do you know about the stink bomb?"

"I don't know anything about the stink bomb. No matter how many times you ask me, my answer's not going to change."

"Maybe you didn't do it, but I think you know who did. I need a name, and I need it now."

"I can't help you."

"Can't or won't?"

"Can't and won't." Bug stared at the agent. "Perhaps you'd like to take me outside and shoot me."

"Don't give me a reason." The fed unholstered his weapon. "You have a bad attitude, Mr. Bugge."

"I just don't like being held here against my will for no reason."

"We're the government, son. We don't need a reason." The agent spoke softly. "We believe the stink bomb was part of a sophisticated plot to embarrass the Vice President."

"The Vice President doesn't need my help. He's an embarrassment all by himself."

"You see, Mr. Bugge, that right there, that's the sort of remark that can get you in a heap of trouble." The agent put a hand on Bug's shoulder. "You don't want a heap of trouble, now, do you?"

"No."

The agent scribbled in his notepad. "By now, the Vice President is on Air Force Two, heading back to DC. I should be on the plane with him. Instead, I'm spending what's left of my night here with you. Do you know how that makes me feel, Mr. Bugge?"

The agent didn't wait for an answer. "You said you were here to listen to the Vice President's speech. What did you hope to accomplish?"

"I hoped to remind the Vice President that the war in Vietnam is an atrocity."

"How did you intend to do that?"

"By being here."

The agent leaned forward in his seat. "Would you like to explain that?"

"When the Vice President gives a speech at a place like this, he looks out at the audience and all he sees are his supporters. People who look like him. People who think like him. I wanted the Vice President to look out at the audience tonight and be reminded that there are Americans who don't look like him, who don't think like him. He can make fun of us. He can insult us. He can arrest us. But we're not going away. This is our America, too."

"So, you really didn't have anything to do with the stink bomb?"

"No. I didn't."

"It was just an unfortunate coincidence."

Bug nodded. "That's right. A coincidence."

The agent was growing tired of the interview. "You're free to go."

"So, you believe me?"

"The federal government doesn't believe in coincidences." The agent smiled. "We'll be in touch."

# 13

IT DIDN'T TAKE LONG BEFORE BUG'S CONFRONTATION AT the VFW spilled over into the ashram.

Willow was having tea when Detective Johnson and two uniforms opened the front door and announced themselves.

Willow approached the officers, polite but firm. "Excuse me, but this is a house of worship. You cannot bring your weapons inside."

Detective Johnson grinned at the uniformed cops. "Does this place look like a house of worship to you?" He looked back at Willow. "It barely looks like a coffee shop."

She measured her words carefully. "I asked you politely, Detective. Now I'm telling you, you cannot come in here with your weapons."

Johnson glared. "I'm looking for George Thomas Bugge."

At the sound of his name, Bug stepped out from the kitchen. "You're not welcome here."

Johnson flashed his badge. "Your friends at the Secret Service send their regards."

"I should have figured." And then, under his breath he added, "Pigs."

"Mind if we look around?" Johnson didn't wait for an answer.

Bug scowled. "Actually, I do mind. So, unless you have a warrant, I'm going to have to insist that you leave."

"You don't own this place, do you, Mr. Bugge?" Again, Detective Johnson didn't wait for an answer. "I spoke with the property owner, a very nice lady by the name of . . ." he pulled out his notepad, "Nancy Harris. Miss Harris has given us permission to enter and search the property. And that is exactly what we intend to do. Now stand back."

Johnson motioned to the uniforms to begin a systematic search. By the time they finished, the front room was in a shambles.

"What's back there?"

Willow followed the detective's gaze. "That's the prayer hall."

Four people sat quietly in the prayer hall, meditating. Emily was one of them. The uniformed officers were especially thorough, ripping open the brocade prayer cushions and desecrating the antique wooden altar.

It was late in the afternoon when the police made their exit. Willow lit two sticks of sandalwood incense. It didn't seem to help. The bad vibes lingered for days.

# 14

WHEN BEN GOT HOME, HIS FATHER WAS SITTING AT THE kitchen table, staring at a piece of paper, muttering under his breath and drinking a beer. His mother stood at the sink, washing dishes.

"How was work, dear?" she asked.

"It sucked."

"Watch your language." Detective Miller slammed the can down, beer slopping out onto the formica table. "Do you ever go to that ashram place?"

"The place on Main Street?" Ben had already heard from Emily about the police visit. "One time."

"Only one time? What were you there for?"

"The brown rice knish. What's this about, anyway?" *As if I don't know.*

"Johnson was there on official police business. This is a copy of his report." He waved the sheet of paper in Ben's face. "That hippie teacher was there. Your girlfriend was there." His voice grew louder. "Do you understand how embarrassed I would have been if you had been there?"

"How embarrassed you would have been? How about, how embarrassed I would have been. After all, I wasn't the one destroying religious artifacts!" Ben was pushing the limits, but he was past the point of caring.

"I don't want you going back to that place."

"I already told you. I was only there one time."

"Then it's settled. You won't go back."

"I didn't say that."

"But I did. Your girlfriend is lucky she wasn't arrested." His voice was low now, little more than a whisper. "I don't want you seeing her anymore."

"I'm not a child. You can't tell me where I can go and who I can see."

"As long as you live in my house, you'll live by my rules."

"That's not fair."

"Enough!" Ben's mother was beside herself. "How long is this going to continue?"

"Until he apologizes," they replied, in unison.

Detective Miller turned to his wife. "See what I mean, dear?"

She looked at Ben. He could see the sadness in her eyes. "Apologize to your father."

An apology was out of the question. "You used to be a good cop." Ben paused. "What happened?"

The detective doubled over like a man who'd just been sucker punched. "None of your business."

## 15

TOMMY CALLAHAN WAS SIX CREDITS SHORT OF AN APPOINT-
ment with the Nassau County police force. In the meantime, he
helped out at the Fourth Precinct. Mostly he made coffee and
ran errands, but from time to time, the Captain let him do "real"
police work. Recently, he'd been allowed to help with the clerical
work, transcribing witness statements and wiretaps.

And that was what led him to breakfast with Detective Miller.

When Tommy got to Sonny's, Detective Miller was sitting at a
back booth, eating a cheese Danish and drinking coffee. He signaled for the waitress.

"Putting on a few," Tommy said in an attempt at cop banter.

Detective Miller might have been offended but didn't react
that way. Instead, he sucked in his gut. "I weigh the same as I did
when I was at the Academy with your father."

"If you say so." Tommy chuckled. "What did you think of the
Vice President? I thought he was inspiring. I'm surprised you
didn't bring your son along to meet him."

"Ben is not a fan of the Vice President. It's one of the things we
argue about." Detective Miller shook his head. "He argues with
me about everything."

"I'm sure it's just a phase, sir. He'll outgrow it."

"But this is different."

"How so?"

"He's been hanging around with a bad crowd."

"That is different. Are you sure? I don't picture Ben joining a gang."

"Not a gang." The detective frowned. "A goddamn hippie."

"Is that all?" Tommy tried to stifle a laugh. "They all want to be hippies."

The waitress came over with a fresh pot of coffee and another couple of cheese Danishes.

Detective Miller waited until she left to ask about the chloroform.

Tommy looked around the luncheonette. "Here's the thing. We're working a big case over at the Fourth, a political case."

"You're working a case?" Detective Miller gave him a funny look.

"You know what I mean. Anyway, the detectives are working a big case. Captain asked me to transcribe a wiretap. Of course, I'm not supposed to talk about it. But if it helps you find a killer . . . Rosalie Bayard was a nice lady. She deserves justice, don't you think?"

"Yes, I do."

"I don't want to do anything that will jeopardize my chance of becoming a police officer."

"I understand. We're just here for the coffee and Danishes."

"Exactly. So, here's the thing. In the course of listening to the wiretaps, I heard something that you might find useful." Tommy Callahan nibbled on a cheese Danish while deciding how much to say. "Do you know Johnny Gee?"

"Of course. He's in Dannemora."

Johnny Gee Senior was a professional killer, well-known to

the Nassau County Police Department. When he was sent to Clinton Correctional, it was rumored that he had unfinished business on Long Island.

"Not Senior."

According to the scuttlebutt at the Fourth Precinct, Johnny Gee Junior had taken over the family business.

Detective Miller shook his head, doubting Tommy's info. "For much of his life, Johnny Gee has been doing odd jobs for his father, some of them legal, some not so much, but none of them, strictly speaking, felonious."

"That's true, sir. But I've been transcribing the case file. I think maybe Junior is filling in for his father."

Over three decades, Johnny Gee Senior had built up a successful business as a killer for hire. He didn't care much about his clients or their targets, as long as they made their payments on time and in cash.

Unlike his father, Junior wasn't comfortable around guns. Senior found that humorous. *Guns don't kill people*, he'd tell his son. *People kill people.*

"When Senior got sent away to Dannemora, he made it clear that he expected Junior to take care of unfinished business. Junior, at the ripe old age of twenty-nine, appears to have hit a crossroads."

"So, what's that got to do with me?"

"Last year, in Lido Beach, there was a dead hooker. The only thing I can tell you is we picked Junior up on a wiretap. In the middle of an unrelated conversation, he made mention of chloroform."

# 16

BACK AT THE STATION HOUSE, DETECTIVE MILLER STOOD
in the Captain's doorway, waiting for his superior to wave him in.

"Can I have a minute, Cap?"

"What is it?"

"Johnny Gee has been talking about chloroform."

"And you know that how?"

"A source."

The Captain looked up from his desk but said nothing.

Detective Miller cleared his throat. "I've been thinking about
the Bayard case as a burglary that went bad, but if the Gees are
involved . . ."

The Captain nodded. "Then it's a homicide. What's your next
step?"

"I've already asked a couple of uniforms to sit on Junior's
apartment. In the meantime, I'm going to pay another visit to
Dr. Bayard."

"Squeeze Bayard if you have to, but tread lightly with Junior."
If the Captain knew something, he wasn't saying. "And keep
me apprised."

✌

The Southern State Parkway was heavy with beach traffic. It took Detective Miller nearly an hour to go the ten miles to Hanover Chemical.

The facility was larger than he expected, located in an industrial park a few miles south of the Nassau Coliseum. There was a security desk just inside the front entrance. He showed the guard his badge and asked for Dr. Bayard.

The guard buzzed upstairs. "There's a detective here to see Dr. Bayard."

"Dr. Bayard's secretary will be down in just a moment."

After quite a few moments, a young woman approached the security desk.

"Hello, Detective. I'm Miss Conaway, Dr. Bayard's secretary. Please accept my apology for the delay."

"No apology needed, Miss Conaway." She was a pretty woman, dressed in a linen skirt and blouse. The skirt was an inch too short for business attire and the blouse too revealing by Detective Miller's standards, but he was old-fashioned that way. She was, he decided, the sort of woman who was unused to making apologies.

"Follow me," she said.

The detective watched the curve of her legs as she led the way upstairs. She stopped at a second-floor reception area and asked the detective to please take a seat.

"Dr. Bayard will be available in just a moment."

As time passed, Detective Miller wondered whether anyone at Hanover Chemical understood the concept of a "moment."

Dr. Bayard came down the hall, wearing a white lab coat over a white shirt and navy blue club tie. He looked remarkably good for a man who'd just gotten out of the hospital.

"Hey. It's good to see you up and about. I must say, I was surprised to hear you're back at work already."

"I'm working on a time-sensitive project."

"That's right. You mentioned a top-secret project. Deforestation, if I remember correctly."

"That's right."

"I seem to recall you said if you told me about the project, you'd have to kill me."

"That was just an expression." Dr. Bayard coughed. "I hope you're here with news, Detective."

"Is there someplace we can speak?"

"Of course. Is anyone using the small conference room, Karen?"

"Let me check the schedule." Karen examined a clipboard on the corner of her desk. "It's available."

"This way, Detective."

Without waiting, Dr. Bayard walked down the hallway. Detective Miller resisted the impulse to catch up with the chemist. Instead, he slowed his gait. *Let him wait.*

The conference room was small, but comfortably furnished. Detective Miller took a seat across from Bayard.

"It's come to my attention that I may have been looking at your case the wrong way."

"What do you mean?"

"I mean, I've been looking at it as a burglary gone bad."

"I'm no expert, Detective, but that's what it looks like to me."

"Only nothing was stolen."

"Something must have scared the burglars off before they were done."

"Yes, that is a possibility."

"Am I to assume you are now considering another possibility?"

"I think this may have been a homicide."

"But the house—"

"Was staged to make it look like a burglary."

"As I said, Detective, I'm no expert."

"No, that's true, but you can still be helpful. Can you think of anyone who would want to murder you or your wife?"

"No, that's preposterous. Everyone who knew my wife loved her. And I know that I can be a trifle annoying, but murder, why, that's ridiculous."

"Does the name Johnny Gee mean anything to you?"

"I don't think so."

"Perhaps you know him as Junior."

"It doesn't ring a bell. Does this Junior character have something to do with the burglary?"

"For now, let's just say that he's a person of interest."

"Well, thank you for coming all the way out here to bring me up-to-date, but if you're done, I need to get back to the lab."

Dr. Bayard got up out of his chair. Detective Miller remained seated.

"Yes, I'm sure you're busy. You know, I haven't been in a chemistry lab since high school. Perhaps you could spare a few minutes and give me the fifty-cent tour?"

"I'm sorry, Detective. The lab is top-secret."

"It might help move the investigation forward, if I knew a little bit more about deforestation."

"I don't see how that's relevant. Please understand, this really is top-secret. We're developing a chemical compound to help our troops in Vietnam."

"A military weapon? I can certainly understand why this needs to be kept quiet. You have my word."

"It's not a weapon, not exactly. Are you familiar with the Viet Cong, Detective? They don't fight fair. We hope to provide our troops with a chemical compound that will level the playing field, so to speak. The military has one already, but we believe we are developing a product that will be more effective. I'm sorry, Detective, that's as much as I can say about the project. I really do have to get back to the lab."

"If you think of a name, you'll get in touch?"

"Of course."

"Thank you for your time." Detective Miller stood up to leave. "You wouldn't happen to use chloroform to formulate your top-secret compound?"

## 17

POLICE OFFICERS KEPT EYES ON JOHNNY GEE'S APARTMENT
for three days. They maintained surveillance even when it became
clear they were wasting time and resources. The Captain pulled
the officers off the surveillance detail.

"Where are we, Miller?"

"There was no sign of forced entry at the Bayards' home and
no report of anything being stolen. Someone wanted her dead.
Maybe the husband. We have a possible link to Johnny Gee Junior,
but he's gone into hiding."

"So, where do we go from here?"

Detective Miller had an idea. He didn't like the idea, but at
least it was an idea. "It's time for me to take a road trip. I'd like to
talk to Senior."

"I don't think you'll get anything from Gee. Still, it's worth a try."

The Captain started to walk away, but Miller called him back.

"What about phone records?"

"The court won't approve a fishing expedition. Get me something solid on Bayard that I can bring to the ADA, and then we'll
talk."

"Begging your pardon, Captain, but I wasn't talking about
Bayard's phone. I was talking about Junior's."

"I'm listening, Detective."

"We know that Johnny Gee Senior was a contract killer. We believe his son may have taken over the family business. We know that he's been talking about chloroform." Detective Miller gathered his thoughts. "Junior has disappeared. I'd like to know who he talked to in the days leading up to the murder of Rosalie Bayard."

"I'll talk to the ADA. Check with me when you get back."

"I can't take Ben with me." Detective Miller looked at his wife in disbelief.

"It's a long drive. He'll be good company."

"But it's official police business."

"The drive's not official business. Besides, it'll give you time to talk."

Ben's mother, apparently, had more clout than the Nassau County Police Department because, less than an hour later, Detective Miller announced that he was taking Ben with him on the long drive to Clinton Correctional.

Dannemora was twenty miles from the Canadian border, in New York, but just barely. Ben and his father talked about baseball, about college, about Mom's cooking, anything to avoid talking politics.

Not far from Albany, where the road turned westward, they exited the thruway and continued north for another one hundred fifty miles. The Clinton Correctional Facility was located on the edge of town, between the village of Dannemora and the State Forest. The complex, built of stone and iron and concrete, loomed over the village like something from a Gothic novel.

It was two o'clock when they pulled up to the gated entrance.

"Remember, you're not here. Not officially, anyway. So, don't do anything to embarrass me. Do you understand?"

Ben looked up at the guard towers. "I can wait in the car if you prefer."

His father took a moment to consider Ben's offer. "No. It might do you some good to see the inside of a prison."

Detective Miller asked for Assistant Superintendent Shephard. The guard directed them to the Administration Building, and after a brief wait, Mr. Shephard ushered them into a private office.

"How was the drive?"

"Long."

"Did you stop to eat?"

"No."

Until the Assistant Superintendent asked the question, Ben hadn't given any thought to food.

"Let me see what I can do." He picked up the phone and asked an aide to find something to eat.

"You're here to speak to Mr. Gee?"

Detective Miller nodded. "That's right. I hope he can help me locate Junior."

There was a knock on the office door. Shephard's aide came in with two peanut butter and jelly sandwiches and a six-pack of lemon-lime soda.

Ben wolfed down the first sandwich.

While Ben ate, the Assistant Superintendent briefed his father. "After I got the call from your captain, I went through the visitor's log. No one has come to see Mr. Gee since he got here."

Ben stared at the second pb and j. His father grinned.

"Go ahead, Ben. They're both for you."

"Thanks." He made quick work of the second sandwich.

"What about mail?"

"Sorry. Nothing to or from Junior."

Shephard arranged for a guard to take them into the cell block. Ben offered to wait in the office.

"Come with me."

Ben walked with his father down the long hallway, prison doors clanging shut behind them.

Johnny Gee Senior was not happy to have visitors. "You're cutting into my time in the yard."

Ben peered into the cell. Senior was scrappy and combative, a small guy with an extra-large chip on his shoulder.

The guard scowled. "Be nice. Detective Miller drove all the way from Nassau County to see you."

"I'm here to talk about your son."

"I don't have a son."

"Cut the crap, Gee. I'm looking for Junior."

"The last time I saw him, he had an apartment in Long Beach. Of course, that was before I got sent to this hellhole."

"He hasn't been back to his apartment in weeks."

"Maybe he's on vacation." Gee gave the detective the once-over. "You don't look stupid, Detective. Are you?"

Detective Miller returned the look. "What do you think?"

"I think you already know I haven't had any contact with Junior."

"Maybe you're right. But I also know there are ways to get and receive messages that never make it into the prison mail bag." He turned to the guard. "Isn't that true?"

The guard nodded his head. "I'm afraid so."

"I drove all this way just to see you. Don't make me regret my decision."

"I'm listening."

"I want you to deliver a message to Junior. Tell him I'm looking for him. I'm going to find his sorry ass. Tell him it will go easier for him if he cooperates."

Gee smiled. A couple of teeth were missing. He rubbed the stubble on his chin. "What's in it for me?"

"What do you want?"

"Look around you, Detective. I can handle jail time, but this is ridiculous. I want to finish my sentence someplace in New York."

"I hate to break it to you, but this is New York."

"You know what I mean."

"Yeah, I guess I do." Senior wasn't the only one ready to say goodbye to Dannemora. "No promises, Gee, but if you get a message to your son, and he cooperates, I'll recommend you get transferred downstate."

# 18

WHEN BEN GOT HOME FROM DANNEMORA, HE HURRIED straight to the ashram. The place was dark, but the door was open.

"Come on in," Bug said. "You look like crap." He tossed Ben a Michelob. "Take a load off."

The beer was ice-cold. "Thanks."

"Willow trusts you, but I'm not taking any chances." Bug's eyes peeked out from half-closed lids. "So, I need to ask. Can I trust you?"

"Yeah."

"If you knew stuff, the sort of stuff that the police would love to know, you wouldn't say anything to your father?"

"Of course not."

"We're planning a rally on the Fourth."

"I know. You're going to levitate the Pentagon."

"We decided to levitate Village Hall instead."

"Can you do that?"

"I think so." Bug laughed. "It weighs a lot less than the Pentagon. Anyway, we filed an application. Maybe they'll grant the permit, maybe not. Either way, we're going to spend the Fourth of July in front of Village Hall, chanting."

There was a noise at the door. Willow kissed Bug. Then she kissed Ben. "You look like crap."

"I already told him that."

She kicked off her sandals and headed for the prayer hall, returning moments later with a joint. "Do you get high?"

Willow didn't wait for Ben to answer. She took a hit and passed him the joint. She gave an amused smile when Ben nearly dropped it in his lap. He puffed on the joint and passed it to Bug.

They locked up the ashram and walked down the street to Willow's apartment. Streetlights on Main Street sparkled and shimmered.

"Check this out," said Ben. "I can do this with my eyes closed."

Bug slapped him on the back. "You're stoned, little man."

"I'm not stoned." Ben stumbled down the street. "And I'm not little."

Willow laughed and took Ben by the arm. "I'll be your eyes."

In the apartment, Willow hunted through a milk crate stuffed with record albums. She pulled one out, holding up the psychedelic album cover. "Have you heard this yet?" She put the record on her turntable.

None of them said anything until the "A" side was finished. "Play it again."

Willow played it again. Bug disappeared into the back of the apartment. Ben was stuck to the floor. "You're stoned," Willow said, stroking his head.

"I am," admitted Ben, giggling.

Willow shimmied out of her blue jeans. The last thing Ben remembered before passing out was a glimpse of her purple panties.

# 19

"YOUR FRIENDS AT THE ASHRAM ARE PLANNING SOME SORT of protest on the Fourth of July."

Ben squirmed in the passenger seat of his Dad's Ford.

"I don't want you anywhere near that place."

"It's not going to be at the ashram." Ben glared at his father. "Are you telling me I'm not allowed out on public streets?"

"So, you know about the protest?" Detective Miller missed the left turn that would take them to the call center in Hempstead.

Ben tried to point it out, but his father waved him off.

"I know." He made an illegal U-turn. "What do you know about the protest?"

"It's not a protest," said Ben. "It's a public prayer meeting."

"It's an antiwar prayer meeting."

"No, Dad. It's a prayer for peace."

"Same thing."

"No, it isn't. Look, can't we at least agree that peace is a good thing?"

"That's not the point."

"Then what is the point?"

"The point is, there may be trouble. I don't want you caught up in the middle of it."

Ben hadn't decided whether he would be going to the prayer for peace. As a child, he had been taught that sin began with a thought. He never understood what that meant until he woke up on the floor of Willow's apartment. Suddenly, his world was filled with awkward relationships. It was all in his head; he knew that to be true. But in his head, Ben had cheated on Emily. He didn't know if he was ready to see Willow and Emily in the same place, at the same time. But he'd be damned if he was going to let his father make the decision for him.

"There's not going to be any trouble. We're just going to stand there and pray."

"That's all?"

Ben decided his father didn't need to know about the levitating. "That's all."

## 20

FOR AS LONG AS BEN COULD REMEMBER, THE FOURTH OF July had been his favorite holiday. He loved the parade, the picnics, the pie-eating contests, all of it. Especially the fireworks. *Who doesn't love fireworks?* When Ben was little, he would be up at dawn, counting down the hours until he could walk to Fireman's Field.

But the war in Vietnam had changed everything. The Fourth of July had become a litmus test of patriotism. The "love it or leave it" crowd didn't understand that you could oppose the war in Vietnam and still love the United States of America, that you could, in fact, oppose the war because you loved the United States of America.

The Prayer for Peace was scheduled to start at one and would continue for as long as it took to levitate Village Hall. The challenge, as a group, was straightforward—according to Bug, they would chant with such purity of spirit that they would tap into the universal consciousness, and by doing so effect the levitation of Village Hall.

Ben's personal challenge was more complicated—to navigate the afternoon with Emily and Willow without making a complete fool of himself. As if that wasn't enough, his father had been assigned to the police detail at Village Hall. Levitating a building seemed simple, by comparison.

Village Hall was located on a hill at the south end of town. When Ben arrived, he was surprised to see a crowd of at least a hundred people preparing for the levitation. He only recognized a few of them. There were hippies from the ashram, of course, but there were a bunch of kids from the neighborhood, and a surprising number of well-dressed adults. His former pediatrician was among them. Also a couple of teachers. He even spotted a member of the Village Board. But he didn't see Emily anywhere.

Bug discussed the plan with a small group of long-haired hippies. The village had approved the permit application, but as a condition of the approval, they were required to remain one hundred feet from Village Hall.

"Make sure that no one does anything to provoke the police," Bug said. "Other than levitating the building. That will be provocation enough."

Someone asked Bug to explain about the chant.

"It's a simple Sanskrit prayer—*om santih santih santih*—which translates to om, peace, peace, peace. We're going to chant until the building lifts free of its foundation and floats up above the township."

Ben spotted Emily walking up the street. She smiled shyly and stopped a few feet short.

"Are you mad at me?" she asked. "Did I do something wrong?"

"Of course not. What makes you think that?"

"I feel like you've been avoiding me."

"I've been avoiding everybody."

Emily put her hands on her hips. "I'm not everybody. I'm your girlfriend."

"Yes, you are." Ben gave her a tentative kiss. "Do you want to go to the fireworks tonight?"

"I want to make the fireworks tonight." She gave him a kiss that left no room for debate. "But first we have to levitate Village Hall."

"Do you think we can?"

She kissed him again. "I think we can do anything."

Ben felt like he was floating several feet off the ground.

"Hey, you two, save it for later. We've got a war to end."

Willow had arrived.

And so it came to pass that at one o'clock in the afternoon, on July 4, 1970, one hundred demonstrators, standing one hundred feet from Village Hall, began to chant. *Om santih santih santih.* Some of them stood silently, meditating on the idea of peace, but most of them chanted loudly.

Ben watched for signs of movement. He thought perhaps the building was starting to sway, but it was only heat waves rising from the asphalt, distorting his vision.

Village Hall stayed firmly rooted to the ground. Bug had estimated that the building weighed one hundred tons. Perhaps he failed to take into account the additional weight of the half-dozen police officers, among them Ben's father, standing on the portico.

*Om santih santih santih. Om santih santih santih. Om santih santih santih.*

There was something deeply moving about the experience. The building remained stuck to the ground, but Ben was floating in the clouds, looking down at a community that was searching for peace. He located himself in the crowd, his left hand clasped in Emily's. As he floated higher, his view grew more expansive. Ben could see young men in rice paddies, up to their hips in mud and death. All of them looked like his brother Billy.

*Om santih santih santih. Om santih santih santih. Om santih santih santih.*

Ben watched as a car pulled up in front of Village Hall. A young woman got out, leaving two toddlers in the back seat. She entered the building. Ben watched as the car began to slide backward down the hill.

Bug sprinted across the street. He jumped into the car as it picked up speed, slamming on the brakes. Cheers rang out from both sides of the street. The young mother ran out of the building. She grabbed her children, sobbing with joy. Ben watched Detective Johnson run to the scene and shake Bug's hand. Then Detective Johnson arrested Bug for violating the hundred-foot restriction.

Nobody was chanting anymore. People were cursing. Shouting. Ben was worried for his father. If half a dozen cops had to control one hundred angry protestors, there was no telling where this would end. He could feel the hostility as it coursed through the crowd.

Quietly, Willow began to chant. *Om santih santih santih.* Emily joined in. *Om santih santih santih.* Rainbow, Dharma, Patchouli, Stoner, Seymour, and Lily resumed their chant. Without thinking about it, Ben started chanting. It spread through the crowd. Anger gave way to resolve. *Om santih santih santih.*

They chanted until late in the afternoon. Although they failed to levitate Village Hall, they did successfully effect Bug's release from police custody. He walked out the front door of the building and declared the Prayer for Peace a success.

## 21

EMILY AND BEN WALKED DOWN THE STREET, ALONE together for the first time in days. For the moment, the troubles of the larger world faded into darkness. Ending the war would have to wait.

Emily unlocked the front door and pulled Ben inside. They stood in the front hall and kissed. Ben slipped one hand under her shirt. Emily let it linger.

"We need to talk," said Ben.

"Not now." Emily slid her hand up the leg of his board shorts.

"What about your father?"

"He's not home."

"But . . ."

Emily tugged at his shorts and at her own as well. She dragged him upstairs to her bedroom. They tripped over each other, their clothes, their bodies, their desire.

"Are you sure?" Ben asked as they tumbled into bed.

Emily licked his chest and groaned. She climbed on top of him. "I'm sure." She was ready for the fireworks.

Two hours later, lying in bed together, cuddling beneath the quilt, all that remained of the fireworks were a few slow-burning sparklers.

"Am I as good as Willow?"

It took Ben a moment to reply. "I didn't have—"

"It's okay, Ben. I understand."

"No. You don't understand." Ben sat up in bed, agitated.

"You didn't?"

"I didn't."

The evidence suggested otherwise. "Are you sure?"

Ben laughed out loud. "I think I would know if I slept with Miss Cooper."

Emily was laughing now, too. "Pinky swear?"

"Pinky swear."

## 22

IT WAS PAST MIDNIGHT WHEN BEN LET HIMSELF IN THE front door. His father was waiting for him.

"I told you I didn't want you going back to the ashram."

It was as if the ashram had come to symbolize every disagreement between the two of them.

"And I haven't."

"You were at the demonstration."

"It wasn't a demonstration. It was a prayer for peace."

"You can call it a damn sock hop, for all I care. You still shouldn't have been there."

"Assemblyman Weber was there. Dr. Spinner was there. Hell, Rabbi was there."

"Watch your language."

"We're trying to end a war, and you're worried about a four-letter word."

They were nose to nose.

"Things nearly got out of control."

"And whose fault was that?"

Detective Miller didn't answer.

Ben folded his arms across his chest. "It was your fault. You and your buddy Johnson."

"We were doing our job."

"You were abusing your authority. You were acting like pigs."

"I will not tolerate such language in my home."

Ben took a deep breath. "Look, you're a good cop. At least, you used to be a good cop. I was ashamed of you today at Village Hall. Ashamed that you were my father."

"Your friend Bug violated the terms of the permit."

Ben stared at his father in disbelief. "My friend Bug saved two little children."

The detective sat down, his head in his hands. "It's possible that Detective Johnson over-reacted."

"We were praying for peace. Isn't that a good thing?"

"Of course peace is a good thing. But sometimes war is the only way to insure a lasting peace. Billy understood that."

Ben didn't know what to say. They never talked about his older brother.

"When Billy was your age, he enlisted. He understood that you can't have peace unless you're prepared to fight for it."

"Billy was opposed to the war in Vietnam." There were some things that could never be taken back. "Billy would still be alive if it weren't for you."

# 23

IN THE MORNING BEN WENT TO THE CEMETERY AT BETH David. It had been four years since Billy died in Da Nang, four years since they put a headstone in the cemetery. In the ensuing four years, Ben had not gone back.

Billy was and always would be Ben's hero. He was fourteen when Billy enlisted. The last time he saw Billy was the day he shipped out. Billy had pulled him aside and made him promise, when the time came, not to enlist.

"I don't understand."

"The world is changing in ways Dad can't accept. I'm just beginning to see that now. But you're young. When the time comes, you'll understand."

Ben cried. "Dad said the war will be over soon."

"Dad says a lot of things. Even if he pressures you, promise me you won't enlist."

Ben was still crying. "I promise."

Billy patted his younger brother on the head. "I need to go now."

"Tell Dad you changed your mind."

Billy shook his head. "It doesn't work that way."

"But you'll come back."

Billy knew something, but he didn't let on. "Sure I'll be back."

He never did come back. Not even his remains. They put up a headstone in Beth David and pretended there was a body buried there. And then, they never went back. But that morning, Ben was surprised to find a small stone sitting on the top of Billy's headstone.

*Om santih santih santih.*

He put another stone on and promised Billy he'd visit more often.

## 24

BUG WAS RIGHT WHEN HE DECLARED THE PRAYER FOR
peace a success. They didn't levitate Village Hall. They didn't
end the war in Vietnam. But they did change the conversation
in Dutch Neck. Praying for peace wasn't such a radical idea after
all. The local paper ran a story about how Bug got hassled by the
police when he rescued two toddlers trapped in a runaway car.
Bug could sense a change in public sentiment about the ashram.
As he went about his day, strangers greeted him now, saying *om
santih santih santih.*

Suddenly, locals were coming to the ashram, for a cup of coffee or tea, but also for a chance to learn more about eastern reli-
gion, enlightenment, black power, and peace. Bug needed help in
the kitchen and offered Ben a job.

"I can start tonight."

"Tomorrow will be fine." Bug grinned. "What are you going to
tell your father?"

"I don't know." Ben frowned. "I guess I can just add this to the
long list of things my father's not happy about."

Bug always said that he was the ashram's dishwasher. And when
dishes were dirty, he was the one who washed them. But he did

a lot more than the dishes. He cooked. He led prayer groups. Some nights, he mopped the floor. Most nights, after the place closed, Bug would disappear into a back room and do the ashram's books. With a master's degree in business administration, Bug could have been a young executive on the corporate fast track, if only he were white.

In his final year at business school, Bug developed a distaste for the trappings of capitalism. He let his hair grow out. He exchanged his three-piece suits for turtlenecks and leather jackets. He would rather do the ashram's dishes than its books, but he did both in the pursuit of enlightenment. As the saying went, necessity was the mother of accounting.

Most nights, Ben helped out in the kitchen. People kept coming in looking for information. Bug asked Ben to organize a counterculture "lending library." For the remainder of the summer, Ben was the ashram's librarian. He located a dozen books that constituted the ashram's circulating collection and arranged the books according to the Dewey Decimal system. Worship, meditation, and yoga were shelved under 204.3. Hinduism, 294.5. Black Panthers, 322.4. Bug thought it was funny and indulged Ben's compulsive need to organize things. He even let Ben create ashram library cards, but he drew the line when Ben tried to impose a twenty-five cent charge for overdue books.

# 25

DR. BAYARD SAID GOOD MORNING TO THE SECURITY GUARD in the lobby at Hanover and took the elevator up one level to his office and laboratory. His office was done in black and white with hints of silver, a modern office for a modern scientist.

Dr. Bayard complimented himself on the décor. It reflected the taste of a man who believed in the power of science. On the wall behind his desk, he'd hung a plaque. *Leave your assumptions at the door,* it said. *Show me the data.*

When he opened the door, Duncan Bayard was surprised to find Karen Conaway sitting on the edge of his desk, wearing a lab coat and high heels. She gave him a quick peek beneath the lab coat, making it clear that she had indeed left her assumptions, and most everything else, at the door.

"I need to take dictation," she purred. "I need it real bad."

"Don't be ridiculous, Karen, we have work to do."

Karen leaned toward Dr. Bayard. He picked up the familiar scent of vanilla on her neck, the perfume he had given her as a birthday present.

"Don't you want me?"

"Not now," he said, stroking her neck the way she liked.

She reached for him. He told himself to step back, but instead took one step closer.

"You're being bad, Karen." But he didn't try to stop her. He never could stop Karen.

"That's right. I am bad. I'm a bad girl." She slid off the desk. "Spank me."

"This is silly, Karen. I can't spank you in the office."

"Spank me," she insisted.

"If I spank you, will you let me get some work done?"

She turned her back to Dr. Bayard and raised her lab coat. "Spank me and I'll do whatever you want me to do."

Dr. Bayard reluctantly swatted Karen's rump.

"Harder."

Dr. Bayard smiled. Work could wait. "Have you been a good girl?"

"No. I've been a bad girl."

"And what happens when you're a bad girl?"

"My daddy punishes me." Karen shifted her position on the desk. "Punish me, Daddy."

When Dr. Bayard was satisfied that Karen had been sufficiently punished, he stepped into his private washroom.

When he stepped back out, his office was clean.

Dressed in a modest skirt and blouse, Karen sprayed the room with air freshener. "We need to talk."

Dr. Bayard didn't need to talk. Talking was just about the last thing he needed. "We've already talked. You must understand that I can't be seen dating you. It's too soon. I'd feel like I was cheating."

"Did it feel like you were cheating when you took me there on your desk?"

"That's different." Dr. Bayard was spared the need to explain the difference when the intercom buzzed on the desk.

"I'm sorry to bother you, Doctor. I buzzed Miss Conaway, but she must have stepped away from her desk. Detective Miller is here to see you."

"Send him up."

Dr. Bayard greeted the detective at the elevator and walked him back to the office. "What can I do for you, Detective?"

Miller smiled. "Right to the point. I like that."

"We're both busy men. No need to waste time with small talk." Dr. Bayard turned to his secretary. "That will be all, Miss Conaway."

Before leaving, Karen Conaway spent a moment straightening a pile of papers on Dr. Bayard's desk. She also adjusted the setting on his intercom.

Detective Miller waited for her to leave. "I'll get right to the point, Dr. Bayard. Last time I was here, I asked you about Johnny Gee Junior."

"You've learned something about this Mr. Gee?"

"Johnny Gee is a hitman. Do you understand what that means? He kills people for money."

"He sounds like a character from one of those old movies they show on late night TV."

"I can assure you, Doctor, Johnny Gee is very real. In the weeks before your wife's murder, Johnny Gee placed several phone calls to Hanover Chemical."

"Hanover Chemical is a very big place, Detective."

"Yes, it is. But Johnny Gee is a hitman. As far as I know, you are the only Hanover employee whose wife was recently murdered."

"Are you suggesting that someone here at Hanover is responsible for the death of my Rosalie?"

"The evidence does point in that direction." Detective Miller watched Dr. Bayard closely. "Can you think of anyone who would want your wife dead?"

"That's inconceivable. Everyone loved my Rosalie."

"Please understand that I have to ask you this. Were you the person that Junior spoke to when he called Hanover Chemical?"

"Am I a suspect, Detective? Do I need a lawyer?"

The detective spoke quietly, the voice of reason. "You are an educated man, Dr. Bayard. I'm sure you understand that when a man's wife is murdered, the police have to rule out the husband as a suspect. And that's all I'm trying to do here, is rule you out. You didn't talk on the phone with Johnny Gee, did you, Doctor?"

"No, Detective. I didn't."

"I'm relieved to hear you say that." Miller scribbled in his notepad. "But someone here did. I'm going to need to speak to the members of your team."

"Of course, Detective. You can use the small conference room. I'll ask Miss Conaway to coordinate."

Dr. Bayard buzzed.

"Do you need something, Dr. Bayard?"

"Please show the detective to the conference room and make sure he has access to everyone on the team."

Miss Conaway proved to be quite helpful. She was organized and efficient. Detective Miller understood why Dr. Bayard would want her as the project secretary. She set up an interview schedule, getting each member of the team in and out quickly, taking a moment before each meeting to brief the detective on the relevant office gossip. According to Karen Conaway, the relevant gossip concerned Mr. Gillis.

"Mr. Gillis is one of the senior chemists at Hanover. He's not shy about telling people he should have been appointed project leader."

"Have there been problems between Bayard and Gillis?"

"Nothing overt. You know how it is, Detective."

"Actually, I don't know how it is. Why don't you tell me?"

"Mr. Gillis does whatever he's asked to do, but only what he's asked to do. And he makes sure to let everyone know about it."

"Well, that does give me something to think about. Thank you, Miss Conaway."

"There's one more thing, Detective." Karen adopted a pained expression. "I don't usually pay attention to gossip, but under the circumstances, I guess you should know. There have been rumors that Mr. Gillis was sleeping with Rosalie Bayard."

Mr. Gillis, of course, denied having an illicit relationship with the late Mrs. Bayard. "I liked Rosalie, may she rest in peace. Everyone liked Rosalie, everyone, that is, except her husband."

"Were Dr. Bayard and his wife having problems?"

"Some people are saying that Dr. Bayard wanted to leave his wife. They say that he was having an affair with a mystery woman and his wife wouldn't grant him a divorce." Mr. Gillis sighed. "Mind you, Detective, under normal circumstances, I don't pay attention to rumor and innuendo, but I guess this isn't a normal circumstance, now, is it?"

The detective agreed with Mr. Gillis. "No, it's not. So, can you tell me who the mystery woman is?"

"I'm sorry, Detective, I don't have a name. Like I said, I don't pay much attention to rumor and innuendo. You might ask Bayard's secretary for a name. She knows all the office gossip."

"Thank you. I'll ask her. Perhaps she can also tell me why people think that you and Mrs. Bayard were having an affair."

"Maybe I should explain."

"Maybe you should."

"One time, at a party, we played pass the orange. Are you familiar with pass the orange, Detective?"

Detective Miller nodded.

"Anyway, Rosalie passed me the orange, and maybe I enjoyed it a little too much. Maybe people could see that I was enjoying it too much, if you know what I mean."

The detective said nothing.

"It was just innocent fun."

Miller could tell this was going nowhere. "Look, Doctor. I really don't care about party games. I'm investigating a homicide. Can you tell me where you were Friday night, May eighth?"

"Certainly. The second Friday night of the month is bowling night. Me, the missus, and three other couples. Do you need their names? Of course you do. Anyway, I bowled a personal best. I saved the sheet if you care to see it."

"That won't be necessary, Mr. Gillis." Detective Miller got up to leave. "Thank you for your time."

Detective Miller strolled down the hall to the reception area. "I'm finished with my interviews. Thank you for your assistance, Miss Conaway."

"If I can be of any further assistance, please feel free to call me." She leaned in at just the right angle to let the detective see down the front of her blouse. When he didn't bother to peek, she scribbled a note and handed it to the detective. "My home number . . . just in case."

## 26

MONDAY STARTED WITH CHEESE DANISHES AT SONNY'S.

It was apparent to Tommy Callahan, watching Detective Miller chomp on his cheese Danish, that he was not a happy detective.

Tommy wasn't a detective, but he wasn't happy either. "Damn them." Normally, Tommy didn't allow himself to use bad language—it was a sign of poor manners and the lack of a proper vocabulary—but circumstances demanded that he make an exception.

Detective Miller waved for the waitress. "A cola and a tranquilizer for my young friend." He turned his attention back to Tommy. "Damn who?"

"All of them." Cheese seeped out of the Danish and landed on his shirt. "The case I've been working—"

Detective Miller shot him a look.

"Well, you know, the case I've been transcribing . . . anyway, they settled."

The waitress refilled the detective's coffee and brought Tommy a soda.

He finished the soda in one long sip before continuing. "Do you believe in equal justice under the law?"

Detective Miller nodded. "Of course."

"Well, I've been transcribing case notes, and maybe I'm not a cop, not yet anyway, but the case doesn't seem like equal justice to me." What he was about to tell Detective Miller could hurt his future on the force, but he owed it to the memory of his father to do the right thing.

"A hooker was murdered, last summer, in Lido Beach. It was all pretty straightforward until the lead detective learned that one of her johns was a veteran, back from Nam. Look, I don't want to say anything critical of the administration, but some of our brave young men, when they come back, well, they're not right in the head, if you know what I mean."

Miller let him talk.

"This kid wasn't right in the head. And his father was an Assemblyman. The lead detective thought the kid had hired Gee to kill the hooker. The problem was, he couldn't prove it."

"Thus the wiretap."

"Yeah. He put a tap on the Assemblyman's office."

"A judge let him wiretap an Assemblyman? There's more to this case than you're telling me."

Tommy stared into his empty soda glass. "It's possible the detective may have cut a few corners."

"Shit. What happened?"

"There was a meeting yesterday. The captain asked me to type up the notes. The DA, the Assemblyman and his attorney, the Assemblyman's son and his attorney, the Assemblyman's aide and his attorney."

Miller sipped his coffee and grinned. "A friggin' reunion of the Brooklyn Law School."

"The attorney for the Assemblyman made it clear that he would seek an injunction to throw out the wiretap evidence. The attorney for the Assemblyman's son reminded everyone that the kid was a war hero in a war that needed all the heroes it could get. The attorney for the Assemblyman's aide suggested that the aide would plead to a reduced charge as long as there was no jail time. He would, of course, resign from the Assemblyman's staff and accept full responsibility. The Assemblyman would write a fat check. Everyone was satisfied—the DA, the Assemblyman, his son and his aide."

"Everyone was satisfied . . . except for the dead hooker."

Tommy wanted to believe in a world where everyone could get justice, even a dead prostitute. "Is that how things are done? Is that equal justice?"

Miller took a moment to respond. "That's how things are done."

"Anyway, now that the case is closed, I need to tell you something." Tommy pulled a piece of notepaper from his pocket, unfolding it with great care. "When Junior disappeared, the lead detective considered the possibility that he'd acquired a new identity. According to the case notes, a guy by the name of Danny Bello may have created a new identity for Junior. He works out of a tattoo joint in the Flatlands."

Detective Miller smiled. "I've always wanted to get a tattoo."

Tommy couldn't understand why anyone would choose to disfigure themselves like that, but if Detective Miller went after Danny Bello, he wanted to be part of it.

"Me too."

# 27

DETECTIVE MILLER AND TOMMY CALLAHAN WALKED INTO the tattoo joint on Avenue J. It was a run-down storefront, on a street of run-down storefronts, in a neighborhood of run-down streets, but it was doing a brisk business. The owner, a young man, inked prodigiously, looked up from his customer's arm.

"Yeah?"

Detective Miller flashed his badge.

"So, you're not here for a tat?"

"Good guess. What's your name?"

"Leo." He put the ink gun down, trying his best to look uninterested.

The kid in the chair started to complain about his half-finished tat.

"Hold your water," Leo said, smacking the kid on the head. Then he turned his attention back to Miller. "What do you want?"

"I'm looking for a guy name of Danny Bello. I was told I could find him here."

"Sorry, Detective. I haven't seen the dude in a couple of days."

Leo snuck a look toward the rear of the shop. Tommy followed his gaze.

"You wouldn't lie to me, now, would you?"

While the detective was focused on the tattooist, Tommy kept eyes on a guy hanging out in the rear of the store. Mid-thirties, heavily muscled, "Mom" inked on one arm and a cobra on the other, he inched his way toward the rear exit.

The guy pushed the door open and ran. Tommy followed him through the shop, out the back door and down the alley. He caught up with the guy on Utica, but he slipped between a couple of cars and disappeared down Flatlands Avenue. Tommy caught him a second time at the corner of Flatlands and Schenectady.

Tommy slowed the guy down just enough for Detective Miller to catch up. The detective slapped the cuffs on their runner and stood there, hands on knees, puffing hard.

The guy smirked. "Aren't you getting too old for this? Whatever you want, it can't be worth a heart attack."

"Look, asshole, I just want to talk."

"Then what's with the cuffs?"

"Why'd you run?"

"I don't like cops."

"Are you Danny Bello?"

"Who wants to know?"

He showed Bello his badge. "Detective Miller."

"Sorry to break the news, Detective, but this ain't Nassau County."

Miller grabbed Bello by the collar and shook him, hard. "If you prefer, we can do this back at the station." He dragged Bello down the street.

"Take it easy, Detective. Maybe I can help. What do you want to know?"

"I'm looking for Johnny Gee Junior."

"Never heard of him."

Miller got in Bello's face. "Listen, asshole. I know he came to see you a few weeks ago. You provided him with phony identification."

"I don't know what you're talking about, Detective."

"I didn't come here to jam you up, but I will if I have to. I want Junior. If you point me in his direction, we're cool. Otherwise, I'm going to put you out of business. And, just for shits, I'll shut down your buddy's tattoo joint."

Danny Bello did a quick calculation. "Okay, maybe you're right. It's possible that Junior came to see me."

"You provided him with fake ID."

"I did."

"I need a name."

"Sorry, Detective. Do you have any idea how many IDs I process in a week?"

"I don't imagine you're the sort of business that keeps records."

"That's a good one, Detective."

"I guess I'll have to drag your sorry ass back to Nassau County."

Bello tried to run, but he was still cuffed. Off-balance, he bumped into a parked car and fell over. Tommy grabbed Bello by the shoulders and pulled him to his feet.

"You're out of time, Bello. If you know something, this is your opportunity."

"I could probably think better if I wasn't cuffed."

"Nice try, asshole."

"He wanted to swap cars. I told him I didn't do cars."

Detective Miller waited.

"I sent him to a guy in Connecticut."

✌

Wednesday morning, Detective Miller was on his way to Connecticut, Tommy riding shotgun. The Southern State Parkway to Cross Island to the Throg's Neck Bridge to Interstate 95. The trip was hellish. They followed the interstate through the Bronx and Connecticut, looking for Swifty's New and Used Car Dealership, just off the interstate, north of New Haven.

They passed a couple of luxury dealerships in Connecticut, large plaster and glass buildings offering the finest from Cadillac and Lincoln. They nearly missed the turn for Swifty's. The auto dealership was disguised as a cesspool. Or perhaps it was a cesspool disguised as an auto dealership.

Before they could climb out of the car, a salesman approached, appraising the 1968 Ford LTD Brougham. "She's a beauty, sir. I can get you top dollar on a trade-in."

Detective Miller showed the salesman his badge. "I'm not in the market."

The salesman handed him a business card. "The name's Darryl. What can I do for you, Officer?"

"We're looking for a guy. He was here a few weeks ago, looking for a deal on a trade-in."

"I pride myself on remembering my customers, Detective. What's the fellow's name?"

"Johnny Gee Junior."

"That doesn't sound familiar." The salesman rubbed his chin. "Of course, I'm not the only salesman."

"Of course."

"Sorry I can't be more help, Detective. Have a nice day." Darryl walked back in the direction of the showroom.

"That's okay, Darryl. We're not done yet."

Darryl was perplexed. "What more can I do?"

"You can give me a look at the sales records."

Darryl laughed. "I wish I could, but we had a small problem last week. A pipe burst in the ceiling. Most of the records were destroyed. What's left is a total mess."

"Still, we drove all this way. So, how about you at least pretend to cooperate?"

"I'm hurt, Detective. Really. You're welcome to take a look at anything you want. But don't tell me I didn't warn you."

Darryl pointed them to a room in the back of the dealership. Cardboard boxes were piled on a conference table. The boxes were water-stained and sagging under the wet weight. The room was damp and musty. Ceiling tiles dangled from the dropped ceiling. "I told you."

Detective Miller had brought Tommy along for a reason.

Tommy pulled a box off the pile. When he removed the lid, the cardboard box disintegrated. The smell of mildew nearly knocked him over. His throat swelled shut. "Can I move this to a room with a window?"

"I'm sorry. This is it."

The salesman excused himself. Alone in the back room with the file folders and the fungus, Detective Miller and Tommy Callahan went through the paperwork. There was neither rhyme nor reason to the filing system. Manila folders were jammed into boxes at random. Tommy made his way through three boxes without finding anything useful. His throat was raw. His nose was stuffed. His face was swollen. His eyes teared up. But it was all in the name of justice. Tommy stepped outside to get some fresh air.

When his head and throat began to clear, he resumed the search for Johnny Gee Junior's paperwork.

It took nearly two hours, but eventually he located a file. On July 12, Johnny Gee Junior sold his '69 Ford Falcon Sport Coupe to Swifty's for a hundred in cash.

Tommy showed Detective Miller the file.

"It makes no sense," said the detective. "Where's the trade-in? He surely didn't leave Swifty's on foot. How come there's no accompanying purchase?"

But Tommy had no answer for the detective. They went in search of the salesman. At the sight of Tommy's swollen face, Darryl smiled.

"Did you find what you're looking for?"

## 28

ARTIE MEHLMAN HAD NEVER BEEN NORTH OF NEW YORK. Never saw the point. He felt like he'd left civilization in the rearview mirror. *Welcome to Breakwater, Maine* the sign said. *Welcome, my ass.*

Artie pulled into town, looking for something to eat. He tried a slice of pizza and spit it out. *That's not pizza. Not real pizza.*

The hot dogs were worse than the pizza. Artie was four hundred miles from Nathan's. *People live like this?*

He could see the Atlantic Ocean and a little sign that said Town Beach, but there was no boardwalk, no sand, just rocks and water. *This has got to be a different Atlantic Ocean.*

A few miles south of Breakwater, he passed the Maine State Correctional Facility in Thomaston. Perhaps he was just being sentimental, but it made him feel closer to his father.

At least there was lobster, just out of the water and available for less than a buck from a guy with a roadside set-up. The lobsterman laughed when Artie tried to dig out the lobster meat, but the old man showed him how and sold him an ice-cold Schlitz to wash it down. Artie decided right away that the old man was okay.

"We don't get many New Yorkers up here," the lobsterman said.

"I wouldn't think so." Artie laughed at the idea taking shape in his head. It was preposterous. "I think I'll stick around for a few days. Where can a guy find a bed around here?"

The lobsterman scratched his whiskers. "There's some nice motels in Camden. Go north another fifteen, maybe twenty miles."

But he'd gone as far north as he was willing to go. "I mean here, in Breakwater."

The lobsterman thought for a moment and then directed Artie to Mary's Boarding Home on Grand.

"Mostly, she rents rooms to men on release from the prison." The lobsterman drilled his eyes on Artie. "You'll fit right in."

"Not me," Artie assured him. "I'm just traveling through town."

The lobsterman smiled. "I reckon she'll rent you a room anyway."

It was a short drive to Mary's Boarding Home on Grand Street. He parked the Dodge Dart on the corner. A sign on the porch announced rooms to let.

A pretty young woman was weeding the flower bed, her brown hair tied back in a ponytail, except for random loose strands of hair that she brushed from her face while she gardened. Artie tucked in his T-shirt and ran his hands through unruly hair.

"I'm looking for Mary."

The young woman stood up. Her knees were caked with dirt, as were her garden gloves. "You found me." She removed one glove and extended a hand. "Mary Townsend."

"Artie Mehlman."

"Are you looking for a room, Mr. Mehlman?"

"The lobsterman sent me."

Mary chuckled. It sounded like a wind chime.

"I have a vacant room on the second floor," she said. "Twelve dollars per week."

"I'll take it."

"Don't you want to see it first?"

"What for?"

"How long are you planning on staying?"

"I'm not sure."

"You're not in trouble are you, Mr. Mehlman?"

"No, ma'am. Just need a place, is all."

Mary Townsend studied his face. "Okay, then. Follow me."

As they entered the house, Mary explained the arrangements. He had permission to use the sitting room to watch television. He was allowed in the kitchen, as long as he stayed out of Mary's way when she was cooking.

"Meals are served on the sixes."

Artie had to think about that for a moment.

There were four bedrooms on the second floor. Three were currently occupied.

"You can meet the other boarders at dinner."

Artie would have the smallest room, at the far end of the hall.

"The third floor is my private space. You are not permitted on the third floor," she said. "Not for any reason."

"I understand."

Mary smiled. "Welcome to my home. I hope you like it here."

"Thank you, Miss Townsend. I'm sure I will."

Artie sat in his room at the end of the hall waiting for supper. He was nervous about his first meal at Mary's. Unfamiliar with the etiquette of boarding house meals, he didn't want to make a wrong first impression. Artie entered the dining room precisely at six.

Mary and the other three tenants looked up from their seats. Trays of food were already on the table. Pot roast. Potatoes. Green beans. It smelled like Easter at Horn and Hardart's.

"You're late," Mary chided.

"I'm sorry. I thought you said dinner was at six."

"I said dinner was served at six. I expect you to be at the table five minutes early." She pointed to a vacant seat. "Since it's your first night, I won't make a federal case out of it. Would you like to say grace, Mr. Mehlman?"

When he was a little boy, his family said grace nightly. Artie always thought it was odd how his father could come home from work, sit down at the table, fold his hands, and say grace.

Artie took his time sitting down, fumbling with the chair while he gathered his thoughts. "Bless this food. Bless this home. Bless each of the mugs who sit at this table that we may be at peace for as long as we are here. Amen."

"When you put it that way, how long will you be here?" The question came from across the table, from a squirrelly guy with a high-pitched voice and a nervous tic. "I have bathroom privileges every morning after breakfast." He looked nervously at Mary. "This isn't going to change the bathroom schedule, is it?" He looked back at Artie. "We can be friends as long as you don't interfere with my bathroom privileges."

"Mr. Mehlman won't disrupt your bathroom privileges." Mary blushed. "Where are my manners? We must do proper introductions." She looked around the table at her boarders. "Mr. Mehlman, that's Roy. Roy DuClos. Next to Roy is Edmund Webster. He doesn't talk much, so don't take it personally. And at the far end of the table, I believe you've already met the lobsterman, Josiah Tuttle."

"Call me Joe."

"Call me Artie."

"Enough with the chit chat," Roy said. "What I want to know is, what were you in for?"

The lobsterman didn't give Artie time to respond. "I don't think he was in for anything, isn't that right, Artie?"

"Remember the rules, gentlemen. Mr. Mehlman is entitled to his privacy. He will tell us about his past, or not, when and if he is ready."

Edmund reached for the pot roast. He took a couple of slices and handed Artie the tray. No one spoke until dinner was finished. Mary got up to clear the table.

Artie wanted to go back to his room, to hide in the room until he figured the place out, but he also wanted to make a good first impression. "Can I help you with the dishes, Miss Townsend?"

"Thank you, Mr. Mehlman, but that won't be necessary. Why don't you go out on the porch? It's a lovely night. I'll bring you a cup of tea."

Mary's Boarding Home had a wraparound porch with a row of Adirondack chairs. Joe was already outside, smoking a Chesterfield.

"Smoke?" He offered Artie a cigarette.

He took the pack. "Thank you, Joe."

Mary brought them each a cup of tea. Joe waited until she was inside.

"You were telling the truth?"

"About what?"

"Your last mailing address wasn't the Maine State Correctional Facility in Thomaston, was it?"

"I can assure you that I have never been incarcerated in Thomaston or anywhere else."

Joe gave that some thought. "But I get the feeling that you have had some personal experience with the criminal justice system."

It wasn't a question, so Artie didn't bother with an answer.

Joe puffed on his Chesterfield. "Just so you don't allow your troubles to follow you here." He blew a couple of perfectly formed smoke rings. "Mary's had more than her share of troubles already, if you know what I mean."

# 29

THE NEXT MORNING, ARTIE TOOK HIS SEAT IN THE DINING room. It was five minutes before six. Artie was alone at the table and confused.

Mary came out of the kitchen with a fresh pot of hot coffee. "It will be so nice having company at breakfast." She poured two cups of coffee. "I'll be right back."

Moments later, she returned with freshly baked muffins and hard-boiled eggs. "I hope you're hungry."

Artie selected an egg, cutting it in half and sprinkling it with black pepper. "Do you have any hot sauce?"

"Do I have what?"

"Never mind." He took a bite of egg. "Where is everybody?"

Mary chuckled. "Roy and Edmund are lazybones. Most mornings, they sleep through breakfast. But Joe's a hard worker. His day starts earlier than most and ends later. That's the life of a lobsterman."

Artie knew less about catching lobsters than he did about shelling them. "It sounds hard."

"Where are you from, Mr. Mehlman?"

"New York." He nibbled on a muffin.

"I've always wanted to visit New York City. The Empire State Building. Broadway. The Ed Sullivan Show. It must be fabulous."

Artie grinned. "It is pretty fabulous. But I don't live in Manhattan."

He told her about Long Island, about Long Beach, Lido Beach, and Atlantic Beach, about Sheepshead Bay and Coney Island. He told her about the boardwalk, about zeppolis. He told her about Nathan's famous hot dogs.

"It sounds lovely. If you don't mind my asking, why did you leave?"

"I guess I needed a change of scenery. Does that make sense?"

"Of course. We all need a change sometimes." She laughed. Again, he could hear wind chimes. "What do you think of Breakwater so far?"

"I like it just fine."

Mary examined his half-empty coffee cup. "Let me freshen that for you."

"Thank you, Miss Townsend."

"You're welcome, Mr. Mehlman."

When he left New York, Artie didn't have an actual plan. He wasn't pointing toward anything in particular, certainly not Breakwater, Maine. His only intention was to leave trouble in the rearview mirror. When he told Mary Townsend that he liked Breakwater just fine, he meant it. Perhaps he also meant he liked her just fine. It was too soon to tell, but he believed it was worth sticking around to find out. Twelve dollars per week was a fair price for room and board, but even at that price, his cash would run short.

That night after dinner, sitting on the porch smoking a Chesterfield, Joe offered him a solution.

"I'm currently a one-man crew," Joe explained. "With a two-man operation. If you're not afraid of hard work, you can start tomorrow. I leave the house at five."

Artie appreciated the opportunity. "But I don't know any-thing about lobstering."

Joe grinned. "You can learn, can't you?"

"I guess so."

"Five o'clock." Joe stubbed out his cigarette. "I know enough for both of us."

Artie got his first lesson the next morning, before leaving the boarding home.

"That's what you're wearing?"

Artie was wearing what he brought with him to Breakwa-ter—black slacks, a T-shirt, and Italian loafers. When they got to the dock, Joe rummaged through his supplies, pulling out a wool sweater, an extra pair of rubber overalls, boots, and a yellow slicker.

"These look like they might fit you. The last guy left them."

The overalls and slicker fit pretty well. The boots were tight.

"I don't know about the boots. My feet are going to hurt by the end of the day."

"Every part of you is going to hurt by the end of the day." Joe laughed. "Those shoes of yours may be fine in New York City, but they don't belong on a lobster boat."

Mary had packed breakfast to go. They were on the water by six. The lobster boat was smaller than Artie expected and packed tight with lobster traps. The deck was slippery from sea water and fish scraps. He was glad to have the boots, even if they were a little tight. The traps were box-like structures, made of wooden slats and netting, rigged so that a lobster could get inside, attracted by the bait, where it would remain until they hauled the traps. Everything smelled like fish. Everything except the lobster. The lobster smelled like cold hard cash.

His first job on the lobster boat was to bait the traps. Joe showed him how to use a hook to attach a piece of bait inside each trap. "We use porgies, mostly, and redfish."

Whatever.

The traps were organized in strings of ten, each string attached to a buoy with Joe's particular colors and design. Joe's marking was a distinctive orange circle.

Artie was surprised to learn that lobstermen worked on an honor system.

"We pride ourselves on being honorable, but we don't rely on honor alone," Joe explained. "There are hefty fines if you're caught hauling someone else's traps. And there are worse things than fines, if you know what I mean."

*Yeah. I guess I do.*

It seemed like they were hauling more lobster than Joe could possibly sell at his little roadside stand. Artie didn't bother asking. He didn't plan to make a career of lobstering. But that didn't stop Joe from explaining.

"When we dock, I'll sell most of these to the wholesalers. Folks will eat these lobsters at restaurants tonight as far away as Boston."

Every morning, they went out on the water, checking old strings and dropping new ones. On a good day, they were back at the dock in time for the lunch business. Joe would go off and negotiate with the wholesalers while Artie opened the roadside stand. On a bad day, they'd stay out on the water pulling strings until the sun went down.

Joe was right about one thing. Well, more than one thing, but one thing in particular. Every part of Artie's body hurt. At the end of the first day, he was too tired to bother with dinner. He retreated to his room at the end of the hall and collapsed on the twin bed. Something seemed out of place, but he was too tired to investigate.

There was a knock on the door. It was Mary. She carried a dinner plate. "It's against the rules to eat in your bedroom," she told him. "But I won't tell if you don't."

He thanked Mary for the food and offered her a seat on the corner of his bed.

"Thank you, but no. It's also against the rules to have a woman in your bedroom."

By the end of the first week, he had earned enough money to pay the next week's room and board. By the end of the second week, he'd settled into the routine.

# 30

THE DAY STARTED NORMALLY ENOUGH. ARTIE AND JOE were on the boat before the sun came up when the engine seized. They would not go out on the water until Joe could swing a new engine.

Until then, Artie was temporarily unemployed. He sat in an Adirondack chair on the porch at Mary's Boarding Home, drinking a cup of coffee and reading a day-old newspaper. He was certain that he'd left the paper on his bed, but when he returned to the boarding home, the newspaper was folded on the bureau. Artie couldn't shake the feeling that someone had gone through his stuff.

He told himself that he was being paranoid, but if life experience had taught him anything, it was that a little bit of paranoia was good for his health and wellbeing. Perhaps that held true in Breakwater, Maine. Perhaps it was an occupational hazard for lobstermen, too.

Who was going through the stuff in his bedroom and what were they looking for? There were only four suspects. Three when Artie eliminated Joe, who had no opportunity. Two when he eliminated Mary. That left Edmund and Roy. Artie was determined to watch them more closely.

Edmund was quiet. Mary told him that Edmund almost never talked, and that seemed to be true, but it was more than that. He was quiet. The way he moved. Like a submarine rigged for silent running. Artie didn't think he was trying to be sneaky. He just was. He was an odd one, that was for sure, but in Artie's estimation, he was harmless.

That left Roy.

Roy was a squirrely sort of guy, the kind of guy who distrusted everyone. He didn't like Artie and Artie was okay with that. Nearly all of his interactions with Roy had followed the same pattern, with Roy obsessing about some anticipated slight, some narrowing of his rights and privileges brought about by Artie's presence in the boarding home. Roy was definitely the kind of guy who would feel entitled to go through another man's stuff.

Joe was down at the dock, making arrangements for a new engine. Mary was out running errands. Edmund sat in the parlor watching a soap opera. When Roy drove off in his Chevy Corvair, Artie decided that turnabout was fair play. He made certain that Edmund was still in the parlor and then slipped quietly into Roy's bedroom.

Artie's bedroom was sparse, functional rather than fashionable, with furnishings supplied by Mary. He expected the same in Roy's bedroom. Except Roy had made an effort to spruce the place up. He had replaced the light bulb in the floor lamp with a black light. One wall was lined with movie posters—Rosemary's Baby, Dr. Strangelove, Dirty Dozen, and Barbarella. The opposite wall was filled with photographs tacked to an oversized corkboard.

Artie took a closer look. The subject in every photo was Mary. Mary hanging laundry in the yard. Mary selecting tomatoes in the supermarket. Mary eating boiled lobster at Joe's roadside stand, melted butter dripping from the corner of her mouth. Mary caught in all manner of private moments. Hundreds of photos, and all of them Mary.

On his nightstand, Roy had a Gideon Bible and a month-old copy of *Playboy*.

Artie slipped out of the room and closed the door.

"Did you find what you were looking for?"

Artie was dumbstruck. "Are you talking to me?"

Edmund looked up and down the hall. "I must be. I don't see anyone else in the hallway."

"It's just you never said anything to me before."

Edmund grinned. "You never did anything interesting before."

"It was just an innocent mistake. I was looking for Joe's room." Artie stammered through an explanation. "He asked me to bring him some paperwork."

"That's not Joe's room."

"Yeah, I realize that now."

"Roy scares me." Edmund chose his words carefully. "You saw the photographs. Do you think he's stalking Miss Townsend? She has enough on her mind without having to worry about Roy."

"The photos are worrisome, I give you that."

"I try to keep an eye on Roy, but I don't like to leave the house. Maybe you can help with that."

"Maybe I can."

They formed a partnership of sorts, their mission to keep Mary Townsend safe from Roy DuClos. Edmund's territory was the house. Artie was responsible for everyplace else. Fortunately, Mary didn't go very far. As a practical matter, Artie was responsible for the town of Breakwater.

Edmund shook his hand and smiled. "We should talk more often."

✌

It was Mary's habit, a couple of times a week, to take a walk after dinner.

Artie had never given it any thought, but that night, after her departure, he noticed Roy in the shadows. Roy took his time, staying well behind Mary and largely out of sight.

Artie stepped down off the front porch. The air was crisp and clear. The wind came in off the water.

Mary headed downtown. When she arrived at a sprawling two-story brick residence, she went in. Roy snapped a picture of Mary as she walked in the front door. Then he wandered off, back toward the boarding home.

Artie approached the building cautiously. A small sign alongside the front door read, Red Sky Convalescent Hospital.

The building didn't look like any of the hospitals Artie was familiar with in New York.

An elderly man opened the front door. "Can I help you?"

"No," he said. "What is this place anyway?"

"This place," the man said, pride swelling in his chest, "is Red Sky. People come here when it's their time to die."

## 31

ACCORDING TO THE NEWSPAPERS, IT WAS THE TWENTY-fifth anniversary of the bombing of Hiroshima. Normally, that wasn't the sort of thing Ben would give much notice, but it was also the Festival for Peace at Shea Stadium. Bug had scored six tickets from a scalper.

Bug handed Ben one of the tickets.

He could tell right away they had a problem. "Do you see the black stripe at the edge of the ticket? It's counterfeit."

"That's not possible," Bug said. "The dude was righteous."

Maybe the dude was righteous. Maybe he didn't know the tickets were counterfeit. It didn't matter. Ben knew. "I saw it on TV last night. I'm telling you they're counterfeit."

Bug was unconvinced. "All we have to do is show up at Shea and act like everything is okay. We'll go through without a problem."

Stoner was skeptical. "That's fine if it works, but if we get turned away at the turnstile, then what?"

Bug was resolute. "We raise a ruckus, and, with a large enough crowd, we push our way in."

Lily and Willow agreed with Stoner, but no one had a better idea. Emily poked Ben's arm. "You go to Shea all the time. Is there a way to sneak in?"

"I think maybe there is, but we have to be there early."

"How early?" Willow asked.

"For a ballgame, a couple of hours. For the concert, I really don't know."

Bug didn't like being second-guessed. "What's your plan?"

"There's a spot in the outfield, by the bullpen. A chain link fence is all that separates the bullpen from the parking lot. If we get there early enough, I think we can hop the fence. Once we get inside, there are plenty of places to hide. If we can stay hidden until they open the gates, we'll be safe."

"What time?"

"I have no idea. The earlier, the better."

It was already midnight.

The train ran twenty minutes late. It was one of the older trains, scheduled for replacement. It would have been noisy and uncomfortable at rush hour, but at three in the morning, they were the only passengers in the car. The train's clatter was subdued; the ride uneventful. They made good time to Flushing. It was a short walk from the elevated tracks to the stadium itself.

At four a.m., Shea was a ghost stadium, shrouded in darkness. They approached the stadium carefully, quietly.

Lily laughed. She tried to stop, but not before her high-pitched giggles echoed across the parking lot.

They froze, anticipating the worst. There must have been a few security guards on duty, but their luck held out. They didn't see any.

Ben located the bullpen area, along the outfield. It was exactly as he remembered, just a simple chain link fence.

Stoner climbed over first. Ben gave the girls a boost. Emily leaned up against him and stayed there for just a moment before clambering over the fence.

Bug slapped him on the back. "Way to go, little man! Now what?"

Everyone looked to Ben for the plan. He took Emily's hand. "We find someplace to be invisible."

Lily had a request. "Can it be someplace warm?"

She was right. There was a chill in the pre-dawn air. They located a storage area adjacent to the concession stand on the loge level. "We'll be okay for an hour," Ben said, "but we don't want to be here when the food service workers start to show up."

Ben had no idea what the timetable was for pre-festival preparations at the ballpark. So, they didn't stay in any one place for very long. They kept to the shadows, staying out of sight of stadium security. After the sun came up, they could hear people milling about, lots of people—ticket takers, concession workers, ushers, production staff, roadies, and security guards. They split up, doing their best to look like they belonged.

Of course, everyone else was sporting a festival ID tag.

It wasn't long before Stoner slipped in with a group of roadies for the James Gang. Bug found a supply closet and donned an usher's jacket.

Lines began to form outside the stadium. The girls went in search of a restroom. Ben hung out on the concourse, waiting for Emily to return.

After what seemed like forever, the girls exited the restroom, deep in conversation, oblivious to the muscular woman in the private security uniform.

Willow bumped into her. "Excuse me."

"Watch where you're going." The guard stared at Willow, who started to edge away. "Hey, let me see your ID."

Of all the rotten luck. The girls needed a distraction. Ben felt like the guy in those old war movies, the one who gives himself up so his buddies can complete the mission. In the movies, the guy always ends up dead. Ben figured it was unlikely the matron was going to shoot.

Ben pretended to lose his balance, and then he really did. He tripped over his own feet and lurched toward a hot dog concession stand. He managed, momentarily, to right himself, hoping to avoid a bad fall, only to twist an ankle and careen headlong into the counter. Hot dogs and mustard packets flew across the concourse.

People stopped what they were doing to watch his public humiliation. Ben managed to catch Emily's eye. Grabbing Willow's arm and nudging Lily, the three girls ran.

The guard turned her full attention to Ben.

"Are you okay?"

His right ankle was already starting to swell. His arm was scraped raw. His face was streaked with mustard. But the girls had escaped. "I'm fine."

The hot dog vendors were yelling, demanding to be heard.

The security guard sighed. All she really wanted was a quiet moment in the restroom. Like the song said, you can't always get what you want. "Let me see your ID."

Ben pulled his driver's license from his wallet.

"I mean your festival ID." The guard produced a walkie talkie and called for back-up.

It didn't take long for the guard to realize that Ben had snuck into Shea. When back-up arrived, they escorted him to the stadium's executive office. He was ushered into a room and instructed to wait. Ben told himself, all things considered, it wasn't so bad. He would act contrite. They would give him a lecture and toss him out of the festival.

Thirty minutes later, two uniformed officers from New York's 110th precinct opened the door and walked in. Ben was charged with theft of services, a class A misdemeanor. The senior officer read Ben his rights. That was when it started to get real.

They took Ben out in handcuffs, put him in the back of the patrol car, and drove him to the station house on 43rd Avenue.

"Listen up, kid. This ain't Woodstock."

"What my partner means is, we're not going to put up with any lawlessness today."

When they got to the station, the officers put him in a holding cell along with a dozen other festival scofflaws. A couple of them appeared to be in bad shape, the result of too many drugs too early in the morning, but mostly they were kids from the suburbs caught with open beer cans or, like Ben, theft of service. Nothing that could be mistaken for a festival crime wave or a descent into anarchy.

Ben took a seat along the rear wall and waited his turn. He was nervous, but not overly concerned. He didn't bother telling anyone that his father was on the job.

An officer looked into the cell. "Ben Miller?"

The officer escorted Ben to a table in the squad room. He asked a few questions. Ben answered as best he could. He told them about the counterfeit ticket. He caught himself before he said tickets, plural. It was just me, he told the officer.

"How'd you sneak in?" the officer wanted to know. Ben told him about the chain link fence in the bullpen area. The officer was impressed.

"You must spend a lot of time at Shea."

Ben explained about going to games with his father and about the NY Giants. He didn't mention that his father was a detective. There was no need to play that card.

"So, anyway, this is what's going to happen." Ben wasn't going to be held over for arraignment. "You'll be issued a Desk Appearance Ticket," the officer said.

The way the officer explained it to Ben, it was sort of like a traffic ticket, except there was no box to check to plead guilty, no option to pay the fine by mail. Ben would have to appear in court, in person, on August 27.

So, he missed his chance to hear Credence Clearwater and Steppenwolf. He missed Paul Simon, Al Kooper, John Sebastian, and Richie Havens. He missed the James Gang. Miles Davis. Johnny Winter. For God's sake, he missed Janis Joplin. Ben hoped the fine wouldn't be onerous. Missing Janis was penalty enough for his misbehavior.

When Ben got home, his father had a different opinion.

# 32

BEN SHOULD HAVE TOLD HIS FATHER AS SOON AS HE GOT home. At least that was what Detective Miller told his son the next morning. Never mind that it was late and he was in bed, Ben should have told him. They were eating breakfast when his mom asked Ben about the concert. "Did you and your friends have a good time?"

"Actually I ran into a bit of a problem."

His mother stopped eating her oatmeal. "Is everything okay?"

"The tickets were counterfeit."

She frowned. "What a shame. I know you were looking forward to the concert."

"There's something I need to tell you."

Detective Miller didn't like to be disturbed until he finished reading the morning paper. He put down the paper and joined the conversation. "Get to the point."

"We snuck in."

"And?"

"And I got caught."

"What about your friends?"

"It was just me."

Detective Miller shook his head in disgust. "What happened?"

"The police took me to the station house."

Ben's mom gasped.

Ben rushed ahead, hoping his father would be satisfied. "I know I made a mistake, but I managed to work things out with the officers. I got a ticket. I'll pay the fine and be done with it."

"Let me see the ticket."

Ben located the ticket in the pocket of his dirty blue jeans. He smoothed it out before handing it over.

His father took one look at the crumpled ticket and scowled. "Do you know what this is?"

Ben knew better than to answer.

"This is what's called a Desk Appearance Ticket. You've been charged with theft of services. That's a class A misdemeanor. You've been ordered to appear in criminal court on August twenty-seventh."

Ben's mother stood in the doorway, listening. "He can't go to court on the twenty-seventh. He has grad school orientation." She looked at her husband, adding, "You have to tell them he's not available."

"He's going to miss orientation. Hopefully, he won't miss the semester." He turned to Ben and repeated himself for emphasis. "You're going to miss orientation. Probably it will all turn out okay, but I need you to appreciate the seriousness of the problem."

"It's okay. I'll go to court and pay the fine. I'll be at Princeton in time for the second day of orientation."

"Maybe. But all they're going to do on the twenty-seventh is arraign you and set bail."

Again, Ben's mother gasped. "Bail!"

"And assign the date for your trial."

Things sank in even more. "There's going to be a trial?"

"Yes. And if you're found guilty, the judge can sentence you to up to one year in jail. It's unlikely for a first offense, but you need to understand that it is possible."

Mrs. Miller didn't want to think about a trial, and she certainly didn't want to think about jail time. "Ben is a good boy."

"He may be a good boy, but he committed a class A misdemeanor."

"What are we going to do?"

"We're going to hire a lawyer. If the ADA is reasonable, we'll instruct the lawyer to negotiate a settlement agreement. I hope you've been saving your money, Ben. Until this is resolved, you should consider yourself grounded."

"That's not fair. All I did was sneak into Shea. You used to sneak into the Polo Grounds when you were a kid."

"That's different."

"How is it different?"

"It just is."

"Well, anyway, you can't ground me."

Detective Miller was not in the mood for an argument. "I'm not grounding you as punishment. I'm grounding you to make sure you stay out of trouble until the court date."

"Your father makes a good point."

There was still one thing that troubled the detective. "When the officers took you in, why didn't you call me? Why didn't you tell them I was on the job?"

"I didn't think you'd want me to."

"What the hell does that mean?"

"Things haven't been so good this summer. Don't you remember?"

Ben's mom remembered. She gave her husband a look, like suddenly this was his fault. Ben shuddered. That look was going to cost him before the case was over.

## 33

KAREN CONAWAY BUZZED DR. BAYARD ON THE INTERCOM. "I'm going home early."

"Is everything okay?"

"I think I'm coming down with something."

"I'm sorry to hear that, Karen. Go home and get some rest. Don't bother cooking dinner for me. I'll eat something before I come over."

*Sometimes he can be such a pain in the ass.* "Maybe you shouldn't come over tonight."

"What's the matter, Karen? Are you contagious? The last thing I need is to catch something."

*Catch this.*

"Karen?"

She resisted the urge to answer.

"Come to my office."

When she didn't, Dr. Bayard walked out to the reception area.

"I realize you're not feeling well, Karen, but this is still a workplace. You're my secretary, and I won't tolerate your insubordination."

"I don't want you coming to my house anymore."

"But we have an arrangement. I pay the rent and you . . ."

"Then it's time we came to a new arrangement. You're not welcome at the house until you're willing to be seen with me."

"People see me with you all the time, Karen."

She began to laugh, but it came out more like a growl. "People see you with your secretary. I want them to see you with your girlfriend."

"We can't have this conversation out here. Please, let's talk in my office."

Without waiting, he walked back into his office. Reluctantly, she followed. Dr. Bayard tried to give her a kiss, but she backed away.

"What's wrong?"

"What's wrong is all we ever do is screw. I want to go places. You know, movies, clubs, restaurants. Public places. I want to be wined and dined."

"I think dinner at your house is romantic."

"Dinner at my house is secret. I'm tired of the secrecy."

"But it's only seven weeks since Rosalie . . ."

Karen unbuttoned her blouse, revealing a new black bra. "Do you like it?"

Duncan Bayard stared into the abyss. "You know I do."

"Make a dinner reservation. Otherwise, don't bother coming over."

"Tonight?"

"Tonight. Or any night." She buttoned up the blouse. "I'm going home."

This time, Karen let him kiss her. Her hand brushed up against him, as if by accident.

"Pick a nice restaurant. I can be very appreciative, if you know what I mean."

Without waiting for a response, she turned and walked out. She could feel Dr. Bayard watching her every move. She stopped at reception, retrieved her purse from a desk drawer, pushed a button for the elevator, and departed without looking back.

Dr. Bayard checked his wristwatch. He was late for a meeting in the lab. The team started and ended every week with a progress meeting. Without Karen, Mr. Gillis would have to keep the minutes of the meeting. Things were difficult with Gillis under the best of circumstances.

The deforestation project was behind schedule, and the team was running out of time. At the end of the month, Dr. Bayard had a meeting scheduled with procurement officers at the Pentagon. He couldn't go to Washington with any loose ends or unanswered questions. The weekly progress meeting was his best hope for keeping the project on track.

He did his best to concentrate as members of the team gave their reports, but Dr. Bayard was distracted by the memory of Karen's black bra and matching ultimatum. When the meeting ended, he had no idea what anyone said. He hoped that Mr. Gillis had taken accurate notes.

The deforestation project was important, but, at that moment, it paled in comparison to Karen's black bra and alabaster bosom. Perhaps she was bluffing.

Of course she was bluffing. Dr. Bayard knew that Karen needed him more than he needed her. One day it would be okay to take her out on a date, but it was too soon. It would look bad if he were to be seen on a date so soon after the death of his Rosalie.

Dr. Bayard drove home. To strengthen his resolve, he poured himself a gin and tonic. He drove, all alone, to Wang's for a bowl of egg drop soup and a plate of chicken chow mein. He rehearsed what he was going to say when he showed up at her front door.

It was nearly nine p.m. when he rang the doorbell. Karen opened the door an inch, leaving the chain latched. Dr. Bayard smelled of cheap liquor and chicken chow mein.

"One day, it will be okay—"

But she didn't let him finish. She closed and locked the storm door. He rang the bell a couple more times before giving up.

It was important that he speak to Karen, that he make her understand.

Dr. Bayard remembered passing a diner a few miles before he got to Karen's. They would have a payphone. When he got to the diner, he sat down at the counter and ordered a cup of coffee.

The waitress sized him up. He was not the only customer who smelled of alcohol, but he was the only one dressed in a suit and tie.

"Trouble with the wifey?"

"Is it that obvious?"

"We only get three kinds of customers at night—teenagers, truckers, and men having marital problems. You're not a trucker and you're surely not a teenager," she said, "but you are kind of cute." She offered him a cruller with his coffee. "My treat. Name's Trixie."

"Thanks, Trixie. I'm Duncan."

Duncan sipped his coffee while Trixie went off to settle up with a group of teenage boys. When she returned, he asked her about change for the payphone.

She gave him change for a dollar and a refill on the coffee.

Duncan Bayard found the payphone in back and dialed Karen's number. She didn't answer. He needed to speak to her. He needed another peek at her new black bra. Dammit, he paid her rent. He was entitled to some attention.

"Did you work things out with the wifey?" asked Trixie when Duncan returned to his seat at the counter.

"She won't answer the phone."

"Did she throw you out?"

"Not exactly. But she won't let me back in."

"What did you do?"

"Nothing." It was suddenly important that the waitress believe him. "Really."

Trixie smiled and stroked the back of his hand. "If you need a place to stay tonight, I get off in a couple of hours."

"That sounds nice, but I want to work things out with Karen."

"I could tell right away that you were a good man. Karen should count her lucky stars to have a man like you." She leaned across the counter and gave him a kiss.

He considered spending the night with the waitress, but he really did want to work things out with Karen. He left Trixie a generous tip, more than the cost of the coffee itself.

It was past eleven when he again rang Karen's doorbell. Keeping the chain latched, she opened the door an inch.

"Go home, Duncan."

"Please. I just want to come in and talk."

"You just want to come in and fuck."

"Is that so bad? That I like making love to you? I know you like it too."

"I do like it. But it's not enough."

"It's too soon. Surely you can understand that. I need more time."

Karen sneered. "Take all the time you need. But until you're ready to take me out in public, you won't be taking me in private either."

Karen shut the door in his face. Dr. Bayard pushed against the door. He could hear the door frame start to crack.

"Duncan!" she yelled. "Before you do something really stupid, go home."

Her scream drew the attention of a police car as it passed by on its normal patrol.

The officer rolled down his window and pulled the car to a stop. "Is everything okay?" He hurried over to the door. "What's the problem?"

Dr. Bayard turned to face the officer. "No problem. I'm having a little problem with the front door, is all."

The door was still cracked open, the chain still locked, Karen still standing inside. "Are you okay, ma'am?"

"I'm afraid my date may have had a little bit too much to drink tonight."

"Do you want him to leave?"

"Yes, I do."

"You heard the lady. You need to get in the car and drive away." The patrolman checked Dr. Bayard's driver's license. "You've had a couple of drinks, Mr. Bayard. Please drive carefully, sir."

The patrolman turned back to Karen. "What's your name, miss?"

"Karen Conaway."

"If he comes back, Miss Conaway, call the station."

Dr. Bayard got in his car and drove off. The patrolman followed him out of the neighborhood.

Trixie was just closing up. She took off her apron and hung it from a hook behind the counter. "I didn't think you were coming back."

"I need a place to stay tonight."

"I know just the place."

Trixie locked up the diner and pointed to her car, a 1968 Mustang. "I drive really fast, so you'll have to keep up."

"What if I can't keep up?"

Trixie laughed. "Then you're not the man I think you are."

Trixie revved the engine. The Mustang screeched as it accelerated out of the parking lot. She was a block away by the time Duncan got his car started. It took him several blocks to catch up. Just as he got close, Trixie blew through a red light. Dr. Bayard held his breath and did the same. Fifteen minutes later, Trixie pulled her car into a reserved spot at her garden apartment. Dr. Bayard managed to pull in right behind her.

"Damn!"

"I told you I like to drive really fast."

Trixie rented a studio apartment in a small complex in Merrick. The carpet was burnt orange shag. The appliances were avocado green. Her bed filled the apartment. There was no place else to sit.

"It must be hard when you have guests."

She threw him down on the mattress. "I hope so."

## 34

ARTIE WAS UP BEFORE DAWN, EAGER TO HEAD BACK OUT ON the water. It had taken Joe all week to arrange for a new engine. Artie was surprised by how much he missed the long days on the lobster boat. He bounced from foot to foot, eager to be on his way.

Joe stood in the kitchen, savoring his morning cup of coffee.

"Relax, Artie. The lobster will wait for us."

Artie checked the wall clock. "But it's almost five."

"Who's in charge here, anyway?" Joe sipped the last of his coffee. "Okay. Let's go."

The sun rose over the water as they prepped the boat for a day of lobstering. The new engine purred. Joe eased the boat out from the dock.

It had only been a week since Joe's engine seized, but Artie was not an experienced lobsterman. After a week off, he needed to re-learn everything. He was clumsy with the traps, tangling the strings and banging his shins.

An hour into the day, he began to find his rhythm. The water was calm, the sun was strong, and the lobster was plentiful. He would have sung a sea shanty if he knew one. Instead, he sang the chorus from every Motown song he could remember.

After six hours, Joe was satisfied with the day's haul and fed up with Artie's tone-deaf hit parade. "Let's head in."

"So soon?"

Joe turned the lobster boat on a course back to Breakwater Harbor.

The wholesalers were waiting on the dock, glad to see that Joe was back at work. They bought lobsters and re-sold them to restaurants up and down the coast. Joe was not their only supplier, but he was the one they liked to deal with. Honest. Reliable. A lobsterman's lobsterman.

As soon as he had docked the boat, Joe went off to negotiate the deal. Meanwhile, Artie set water on to boil and opened Joe's roadside stand. He boiled a half-dozen lobsters, prepped the spicy mayonnaise, and lightly toasted the buns. Before he could finish the prep, customers were lined up for Joe's Famous Lobster Rolls.

Finally, there was a break in the action. Artie rubbed his neck, stretched his back, and poured himself a large glass of lemonade. That was when he noticed Roy, standing in the shade of a maple tree. He was surprised when Roy came over and ordered a lobster roll. He sat down at a picnic table alongside Joe's stand and picked at the lobster. Artie wondered what Roy was up to.

After a while, Roy waved him over. There were no more customers waiting for service. Artie joined Roy at the picnic table.

"The lobster is good today."

"Yeah."

"Is Joe around?"

Artie pointed to Joe, on the dock chatting with the wholesalers.

"That's okay. You're the one I want to talk to."

"Okay, talk."

But Roy didn't say anything. He picked at the remains of his lobster roll.

Artie had no patience for Roy. "So, what do you want to talk about?"

"Edmund," he said. "He's a strange one, don't you think?"

"Yeah, I guess so."

"Has he talked to you yet?"

Artie was not about to let on. "No. Not a word. How about you?"

"Sometimes. A couple of days ago, he pulled me aside and told me he thought you were dangerous." Roy's head was turned at a forty-five degree angle, but his eyes looked straight at Artie. "Are you, Mr. Mehlman? Dangerous, that is?"

Artie was flabbergasted. "Of course not."

"I'm glad to hear that. He asked me to keep an eye on you."

"Is that what you're doing here now? Keeping an eye on me?"

Roy looked around. "I think Edmund's the dangerous one. And maybe Joe. I haven't decided about Joe yet."

Joe had finished with the wholesalers and was on his way to the roadside stand. Roy jumped up. "Anyway, I've got to be on my way. Don't forget what I said about Edmund."

Joe joined Artie at the picnic table. "What was that about?"

"Damned if I know."

Joe slapped him on the back. "Well, anyway, I got a great price for the lobster. Let's call it a day."

When they got back to the boarding home, Mary was busy in the kitchen. "We're having chicken pot pie. Go clean yourselves up while I get everything on the table."

No one said anything during dinner. Mary tried repeatedly to engage the men in conversation. She got one-word answers, or nothing at all. "I guess I got a houseful of Edmunds tonight."

Artie started to say something about the day's catch, but Joe gave him a look and he stopped mid-sentence, asking instead for someone to pass the biscuits.

When dinner was over, Artie stepped out on the porch for an evening cigarette. After she finished the clean-up, Mary stepped outside.

"I'm going for a walk," she said. "Don't get into any trouble while I'm gone."

"I'll try." The thing was, Artie couldn't figure out who in the boarding home was trouble. Maybe they all were. He stopped Mary halfway down the steps. "Is it safe for a young woman in Breakwater to be out for a walk alone after dark?"

Mary snorted. "Don't be silly. Maybe it's not safe in that town you come from, but here in Breakwater I'll be fine."

"Still, I'd feel better if you had an escort."

Mary blushed. "Do you want to walk with me? How do I know that I'll be safe with you?"

It was Artie's turn to blush. "I . . ." *I don't know what to say.*

"Thank you, Artie, but I don't need a bodyguard." Mary walked down to the sidewalk.

"That's okay. To be honest, I don't want to be your body-guard." He smiled at Mary. "But I would like to be your friend."

Mary returned the smile. "In that case, I'd like the company. I'll admit to having a soft spot for honest gentlemen."

Artie stubbed out his Chesterfield and joined Mary on the sidewalk. "Which way are we going?"

Without bothering to answer, Mary took off toward downtown Breakwater.

Artie was still standing in front of the boarding home.

"Are you coming?"

They strolled past the old homes and into the downtown area. Most of the stores were closed for the night. Some were closed permanently.

"So, what do you think of our little town?"

"I think I like it here."

"Do you think you might stay?"

Artie had been asking himself that very same question. "I think I might. I think I like lobstering."

"Is there anything else about Breakwater that you like?"

Artie measured his words carefully. "I like your chicken pot pie."

"You do know how to sweet-talk a woman."

Mary took his hand. They walked hand-in-hand and said nothing.

Mary turned down a street that Artie didn't recognize. Two more turns, and they stopped in front of Red Sky Convalescent Hospital.

"Would you be a doll and wait for me out here?"

"What is this place?"

"This is Red Sky."

As if that were a sufficient answer.

Mary shushed him before he could ask again. "I'll only be a few minutes." Mary opened the old wooden door and let herself into the foyer.

While Artie waited, he examined the old manse. It was a large two-story residence made of stone and brick. Upstairs, he counted ten windows across the front of the house. He examined a sign by the front door—Red Sky Convalescent Hospital. Nothing about the place made sense.

But when he stopped to think about it, nothing about Breakwater made any sense, starting with his being here. Perhaps when he figured out who Artie Mehlman was, everything else would come into focus.

Figuring that out would take time.

Mary walked out the front door and gave him a peck on the cheek. "Thanks for waiting."

Artie was surprised when Mary didn't head straight back to the boarding home. She walked down to the harbor. The sky teemed with stars.

"Do you know the constellations?"

"Not really."

She pointed vaguely northeast. "That's Ursa Major."

It took Artie a minute before he recognized the Big Dipper. "Okay, I see it."

"Now pan to your left. Do you recognize anything?"

"Is that the Little Dipper?"

"That's great. And if you look a little further northeast, you can see Cassiopeia."

Artie laughed. "Maybe you can see Cassiopeia. All I see is stars."

"That's okay. You did fine for your first astronomy lesson." Mary pointed to a bench on the dock. "Would you like to sit?"

"I'd like that just fine."

They sat on the bench, each lost in their own thoughts and perhaps in each other's thoughts as well.

"Do you believe that people have a right to die?"

Artie tried to puzzle out the meaning of Mary's question. "Begging your pardon, but I don't think any of us have much say in that. When the good Lord decides it's our time, He takes us."

"But if it is your time, if you know it's your time, don't you think you should be allowed to control how your life ends?"

"Are you referring to suicide?"

"Of course not. It's a sin to commit suicide." She searched for the right words. "Maybe you have an incurable disease, you know, cancer or something like that. You're going to die. It's only a matter of when. Meanwhile, what's left is nothing but constant pain. No one should have to live like that."

"I don't know."

"Or maybe it's not your body that is failing. What if it's your mind? Do you believe in an eternal soul?"

"Yes. I think I do."

"And when a person dies, the soul leaves the body. Finally, the body is nothing more than an empty shell."

"I guess so."

"Do you think it's possible for the soul to leave the body too soon?"

"I don't understand."

"What if a person is dying . . . I mean, he's not dead yet, but it's getting close and the soul sort of miscalculates . . . leaves a little early?"

Artie didn't have an answer.

"Tell me about Long Beach. What would you be doing right now?"

"I might be sitting on a bench like this. Only the bench would be on the boardwalk."

"What's that like?"

"On the street side of the boardwalk is the town of Long Beach. Apartments, pizza places, neighborhood bars, surf shops, the bustle of everyday life. On the beach side, there's nothing but sand, and beyond the sand, the Atlantic Ocean. As far as a person can see, nothing but sand and water."

"When you're sitting on a bench in Long Beach, are you by yourself?"

"Well . . . I . . ." Artie could feel the heat rising on his cheeks. He turned away in embarrassment. When he turned back, Mary too was blushing.

"I'm sorry, Artie. You don't have to answer. I've got no right to ask."

# 35

DR. BAYARD WOKE UP ON SATURDAY MORNING IN WHAT was either a very large bed or a very small room. Of which, he couldn't be certain. He rolled over, and just in time, before he murmured Karen's name, he remembered the waitress.

Trixie. They had fallen into bed well past midnight. Trixie had spent the next few hours showing him things he'd only ever read about and a few he hadn't.

Dr. Bayard had only been with two women before, his late wife Rosalie and his girlfriend, Karen. Rosalie had been his high school sweetheart, his first lover, and his steadfast friend until the day she died. Her lovemaking had been unimaginative but reliable. The scientist in him valued her reliability.

And then one day at the lab, shortly after he had selected her to be the project secretary, Karen Conaway had stepped into his office and locked the door. Dr. Bayard remembered the day like it was yesterday.

"If I'm going to be a member of the team," she said, "then I need to be fully committed to the idea of deforestation. Don't you agree?"

"Yes, yes, of course." Dr. Bayard didn't pay attention until Karen unbuttoned and stepped out of her skirt.

She was not wearing panties. And she was totally, as he put it, deforested.

Dr. Bayard couldn't stop himself. Maybe, if he hadn't looked, things would have been different, but he did look. "You're right, Karen. No way the Viet Cong could hide in there."

Dr. Bayard made love to Karen in the office and at the house he rented for her. For three years, he cheated on Rosalie. It was, he told himself, the hardest thing he'd ever done.

Now Rosalie was dead and Karen was his still-secret girlfriend. Or she had been, up until she locked him out of the house. Within hours, he was cheating on Karen with Trixie. Perhaps the waitress was his new secret girlfriend.

It was nearly noon by the time they climbed out of bed. Trixie was, he decided, less pretty in the daylight, but she was not without her charms. She pushed the Murphy bed up into the wall and set out a couple of folding chairs.

"Do you want a cup of coffee?"

"No. I need to be going. You know."

"The wifey."

"Yeah."

Trixie gave him a kiss. "Thank you."

Dr. Bayard wasn't sure what she had thanked him for, but he took pride in his good manners. "You're quite welcome."

Trixie laughed. "You don't even know what I thanked you for, do you?"

"Not really. Maybe. Sort of."

"Most married men need to make excuses before they hop into bed. And again when they're finished. They want to tell you their sob story, how the wife doesn't understand them. I guess it helps them justify the cheating. But you, with you it was just sex." Trixie paused. "I'm not going to see you again, am I?"

He reddened. "No. Probably not."

"Well, if you have another fight with the wifey, you know where to find me."

"I'd like that." He knew right away that didn't sound right. "I don't mean I'd like to have another fight with my wife. I guess I just mean, I had fun."

"I had fun with you, too." Trixie grinned. "Just so you understand, you can come see me again whether or not you have a fight with the wifey."

Dr. Bayard pulled on his clothes and left.

Trixie was late for her Sunday shift at the diner.

Driving home to Dutch Neck, Dr. Bayard considered his options. Karen had given him an ultimatum. It would be unseemly to be seen dating so soon after Rosalie's passing, but a spiteful Karen could cause all sorts of mayhem at the lab and at home. Perhaps, if he was careful, they could spend a little well-planned time together in public. Not too often and not too close to home, but it might be enough to satisfy Karen.

Trixie had been right about one thing. Their hook-up was just about sex. With Karen, it was about more than sex. Dr. Bayard knew himself to be a complicated man, with complicated needs. Karen listened. She understood him. In the three years that he had been cheating, even Rosalie had noticed the difference. Just a few weeks before she died, Rosalie had commented that the last couple of years had been the best years of their marriage.

Rosalie had been happy. That had to count for something.

The first thing he did when he got home was make a dinner reservation. The second thing he did was send Karen a dozen long-stemmed red roses. The third thing he did was take a very long, very hot shower.

It was mid-afternoon when Karen called. The roses had arrived, and on the card was the information for that evening's dinner plan at a romantic restaurant overlooking Long Island Sound. The tiny waterfront restaurant was just the sort of place where he could repair the damage in their relationship, and it was far enough from home to be safe.

"I'll pick you up at five," he said. "Pack an overnight bag."

"Overnight!" Karen squealed with delight. She had just enough time to go to the mall and shop for a new outfit.

Two new outfits, as it turned out, a little black dress and a red low-cut number that accentuated her ample bosom. Dr. Bayard would enjoy choosing. He deserved to make the selection. After all, she paid for the two outfits with one of his credit cards.

# 36

DR. BAYARD RANG KAREN'S DOORBELL. SHE OPENED THE door, threw her arms around him, and gave him a big, wet kiss. She wore red high heels, red lipstick, and nothing else.

"Karen!" He pushed her inside and shut the door. "The neighbors might see!"

"I'm all packed," she said, pointing to a matching suitcase and make-up case.

"You look beautiful. But really, Karen, you need to put some clothes on."

Karen had another idea. "This won't take long."

And it didn't.

Twelve minutes later they were in the car, heading for the North Shore.

"Tell me again where we're going?"

"Port Jefferson."

It was barely twenty miles from the Atlantic Ocean to Long Island Sound. Less than twenty miles, but worlds apart. Long Islanders lived their lives on the South Shore or on the North Shore, rarely crossing the midline. Dr. Bayard was counting on it.

He checked his watch. "We're twelve minutes behind schedule." He pressed down on the gas pedal, accelerating past an unmarked police car.

The officer waved him to the curb.

"License and registration, sir."

"I'm sorry, officer, I'll slow down."

"Please sir, your license and registration."

The officer handed him a speeding ticket. "I clocked you doing sixty-three in a forty-five. I wrote you up for doing fifty-three."

"Thank you, officer."

Dr. Bayard put the car in drive and accelerated slowly into traffic. He re-checked his watch. They were twenty-five minutes late.

Karen waited until the officer was gone before saying anything. "You can be so impatient sometimes."

"Are you talking about my driving?"

"That, too. You need to learn how to slow down."

Dr. Bayard said nothing until he pulled into the motel parking lot. "We're here."

The sun was going down, the sky tinged with purple and pink. Sailboats bobbed at anchor in the harbor.

Dr. Bayard found a bellman to help with the luggage. He stopped at the desk to check in. Karen peeked over Duncan's shoulder. *Mr. and Mrs. Smith.* Karen wasn't happy about the Smith, but she was thrilled by the Mr. and Mrs. She gave him a hug in the lobby. By the time they got to the room, the bellman had delivered the luggage.

"We can unpack later. We're going to be late for our dinner reservation."

"Don't be silly. I need time to change and do my make-up."

Karen took the new dresses out of the suitcase and held them up for Dr. Bayard's consideration. "Do you like them?"

"Like them? I love them."

"I'm so glad. I put them on your credit card."

"I'll call the restaurant and see about a later table."

The restaurant was situated adjacent to the motel. They got a table in the rear. The wall was floor-to-ceiling glass, with an extraordinary view of the harbor.

"This is lovely," Karen said, and meant it. "Thank you."

She ordered the petit filet. Duncan chose the surf and turf and a bottle of Bordeaux. When the sommelier uncorked the wine, he offered Duncan a taste. He swirled the wine and took a sip. "Very nice."

The sommelier poured two glasses.

"To us," said Dr. Bayard.

"To us," echoed Karen.

It was nice, Dr. Bayard decided. After all the sex, they were on a first date.

"When you were a little girl, what did you want to be?"

"You mean, when I grew up?"

Duncan sipped the Bordeaux and nodded his head. "Yes, when you grew up."

"I wanted to be a figure skater, but when I hit puberty, I discovered I had too much figure to be an Olympic skater, if you know what I mean."

"I know what you mean." He stared at Karen in the red dress. "I bet you were good."

"State champion."

"That's amazing. How come I never knew that about you?"

"You never asked."

"What else don't I know about you?"

Karen didn't bother to answer.

After dinner, they took a long walk along the harbor. Sailboats lined the dock. The wind was coming in off the water.

"I have a meeting in Washington on the twenty-sixth."

Karen kept his calendar. She knew all about his meeting at the Pentagon. "Let's not spoil things by talking about work."

"I'm sorry. What I meant was, maybe you could come with me. We could spend a few days together."

"Do you mean, I could be there like a secretary or like a girlfriend?"

"Like a girlfriend, mostly."

Karen threw her arms around him. "I would love that."

"Maybe just a little bit like a secretary."

Karen didn't mind a little bit. After all, Hanover was footing the bill. She slipped her hand between his legs. "Would you like to go back to the room?" It was a rhetorical question.

But when they got back to their room, nothing happened. Duncan wanted to, but he couldn't seem to rise to the occasion.

"That's never happened to me before."

"It's okay. We don't have to do it. Sometimes it's nice just to cuddle."

Dr. Bayard fell asleep cuddling with Karen, but thinking about the waitress, Trixie.

He slept poorly. Karen had been more than understanding. In truth, Dr. Bayard would have preferred if she had gotten angry. Her anger might have been just the thing he needed. Instead, he dreamt about Trixie and woke up aroused. He was ready to leave the night's failure behind them.

Karen was in the mood to be agreeable. "When you fall off a horse . . ."

He was eager to climb back on. But once he got himself settled comfortably, so to speak, the cinch strap went limp, and he slipped off the saddle.

Duncan tried to tell her it had never happened before, but this was the second time in less than twelve hours. There was no telling where this might lead. Dr. Bayard pictured himself in Washington, DC. He imagined a successful meeting with the procurement officers at the Pentagon. He imagined a celebratory dinner at a fancy Georgetown restaurant. He imagined going back to their DC hotel and being unable to complete the celebration.

He took a shower, packed his suitcase, and waited impatiently for Karen. "It's check-out time."

Karen understood what was bothering him, to the extent that a woman can. But she had needs, too. "Can't we have breakfast first? It's a long drive home on an empty stomach."

"I want to get on the road."

"Don't be silly. We're going next door and having poached eggs."

Dr. Bayard bit his tongue and followed Karen to the restaurant.

The view from the windows was still spectacular. The sun was shining. The harbor bustled with activity. Sailboats tacked as they made their way out past the point.

Karen ordered eggs benedict. Under the table, she slipped off a shoe and ran her foot along the inside of his thigh.

Duncan finished his eggs and waited for her to do the same.

Karen wiped the hollandaise from her lips and jumped up from the table. "Don't worry, Duncan. I had a wonderful time regardless."

## 37

ON SUNDAY, THE ROUTINE AT THE BOARDING HOME WAS different. Mary and Joe spent the morning at the local Presbyterian Church. They were gone by the time Artie came downstairs. Roy left the house as well. Artie considered following him, but Mary was safe in church with Joe. Roy wouldn't bother her there. Instead, Artie went into town for a fried egg and a cup of coffee. He read the local paper and wondered what might be happening in Long Beach.

When he returned to the boarding home, Edmund was sitting on the porch, sipping a glass of iced tea and reading a magazine.

"Good morning, Artie."

For the second time since Artie moved into Mary's, Edmund was in the mood to talk.

"You went for a walk last night with Mary."

"Yes."

"Do you think that's a good idea?"

"As I recall, you were the one who asked me to keep an eye on her."

"That's true. I did ask you to keep an eye on her. As you know, I am worried about Roy. Should I also be worried about you, Artie Mehlman?"

Artie liked Edmund better when he wasn't talking. "It was just a friendly walk. Mary taught me the constellations."

"And what did you teach our Mary?"

Artie felt the muscles tighten in his jaw. "I'll ask you to mind your own business."

"I'm sorry, but it is my business, Artie Mehlman from Long Beach, New York. Did you tell our Mary all about New York?"

Something in Edmund's tone of voice sent shivers down Artie's spine. "What are you getting at?"

"Some folk assume that because I don't talk much, I must be stupid. Are you one of those people, Mr. Mehlman? If you know what's good for you, you won't underestimate me."

"I think we're done here." Artie started to walk away.

"Not so fast." Edmund smiled broadly. "The interesting thing is, there is no record of an Artie Mehlman in Long Beach, New York."

"Of course there is." Artie sat down in one of the Adirondack chairs.

"I contacted the DMV in New York. They haven't issued a driver's license or a vehicle registration to anyone by the name of Artie Mehlman. By the way, your car has Connecticut plates." Edmund rubbed his hands together as he spoke. "But I'm sure you have an explanation."

"Yes, I do." But he chose not to offer one.

Edmund wasn't finished. "I contacted the Board of Elections. Artie Mehlman isn't registered to vote in Long Beach or anyplace else in New York."

"I am, by nature, a private person. I prefer not to share personal information with the government. You, of all people, should understand that."

"Are you hiding something, Artie?" Edmund grinned. "An innocent person has nothing to hide."

Artie jumped to his feet. "I've had just about enough of your prying! My private life is my own business."

"Maybe it is and maybe it isn't."

Artie stared hard at Edmund. Only a matter of a few inches separated them. "Who are you anyway?"

"My name is Edmund, and I am a collector of secrets."

"A collector of secrets . . . what's that?"

"I don't talk very much, but I do listen. I gather information . . . secret information."

"Why?"

"Isn't it obvious?" Edmund chuckled. "Information is power. Secret information is super power."

"What do you want from me?"

"Nothing, really." Edmund rubbed his brow. "Keep an eye on Roy. That's all. And keep your distance from Mary."

"Okay, then, Mr. Keeper of Secrets, what's the scoop about Mary?"

For the first time since arriving at the boarding home, Artie saw something almost human in Edmund's eyes. "Some secrets are meant to be kept close. Perhaps one day our Mary will tell you her story."

As if on cue, Mary and Joe returned from church. Joe headed inside to change out of his "go to church" clothes. Mary lingered on the porch for just a moment.

"Good day, gentlemen."

Artie said hello. Edmund said nothing.

Mary went inside to cook. On Sundays, she served dinner at two.

Artie and Edmund were alone again. "I don't know who you are, but you're not Artie Mehlman."

Artie didn't bother to protest. "What are you going to do about it?"

"Nothing. Nothing at all. Some people collect stamps. Others collect coins. I collect secrets. Consider it my hobby." Edmund paused. "Can I offer you a bit of advice?"

Artie nodded.

"It's obvious that you're hiding from someone or something. Maybe the others don't see that yet, maybe they don't care, but it's my hobby to notice these things. Anyway, it wasn't very hard for me to find the flaws in your current identity. Keep in mind, my only motivation here is idle curiosity. The people that you're hiding from—"

Edmund stopped mid-sentence as Mary pushed the door half-open.

"Dinner is on the table, gentlemen."

## 38

DETECTIVE MILLER ORDERED THE USUAL—A CUP OF COF-
fee and a cheese Danish. Somehow, Tommy Callahan had turned
these breakfast meetings into a weekly routine. It wasn't that
Tommy hadn't proven himself useful; he had. But Detective
Miller didn't like to meet weekly with anyone. He was on his second Danish when Tommy arrived.

Tommy ordered a cola and a corn muffin and waited for the
detective to give him permission to speak.

"I've been thinking about Swifty's. Junior didn't leave there on
foot."

Detective Miller nodded. "Junior bought a car at Swifty's. I can
feel it in my gut."

Miller chomped on the cheese Danish. Tommy picked at the
corn muffin.

"Did we miss something?" Tommy asked. "Junior sold his car
at Swifty's. We have the paperwork."

Detective Miller put down the cheese Danish. An idea took
shape in his head. "If Gee went to the trouble to get a phony ID,
why is Junior's name on the bill of sale?"

Tommy nodded. "The car was titled in his name."

"Exactly." Detective Miller sipped on his coffee, waiting to see
if Tommy would connect the dots.

"Of course." Tommy smacked his head.

Detective Miller stuffed what was left of the cheese Danish in his mouth. "We need to pay another visit to Swifty's."

It was midday when they pulled into Swifty's lot. Detective Miller popped out of the driver's seat. "Remember me?"

Darryl groaned. "How can I help you today, Detective?"

"Junior sold you his car on July twelfth. We need to see the paperwork on every sale you made that day."

Tommy climbed out the passenger side, carrying a portable fan.

"I see you came prepared." Darryl chuckled. "Go ahead. Knock your socks off."

They made their way back to the file room. The room was stacked high with damp, moldy boxes teetering in unsteady piles. It seemed like the boxes had multiplied since their first visit. Detective Miller appreciated his decision to let Tommy tag along.

It took most of the afternoon as Tommy made his way, methodically, through the cardboard piles. The fan made the atmosphere tolerable. It didn't stop his throat from swelling shut, but it did slow the process. It was a tedious task, but Tommy knew it would be worth the trouble if he could help Detective Miller locate Johnny Gee Junior.

Finally, he stumbled upon paperwork for three used car sales made on July 12. Rebecca Jones, from Waterbury, Connecticut, age twenty-one, bought a Chevelle. Albert Becker, from Port Chester, New York, age forty-three, purchased a Volkswagen. Artie Mehlman, from New Haven, age twenty-nine, purchased a Dodge Dart.

Tommy noticed something odd in Mehlman's paperwork and showed it to the detective. According to the temporary registration for the Dart, Artie Mehlman's home and Swifty's New and Used Car Dealership shared a common address.

Detective Miller grinned. "It's time to have another chat with Darryl."

"Can you explain this?" Tommy waved the moldy paperwork in Darryl's face.

Darryl barely looked at the moldy papers. "Sometimes, we get a buyer who is uncomfortable giving the DMV his real address."

Detective Miller took over. "And that doesn't cause you any concern?"

"Here at Swifty's, we pride ourselves on putting every customer in the car of their dreams."

It was hard to imagine that a '67 Dodge Dart was the car of anyone's dreams. "Really?"

"Hey, I work on commission. If someone wants a car, it's my job to make sure he gets it."

"I'll need a copy of the Mehlman paperwork."

"I'm sorry. That's beyond my pay grade."

Detective Miller smacked the table hard. "I said, I need a copy of the paperwork."

Darryl was getting fidgety. "Since the water pipes burst, we don't really know what records we have anymore. So, we wouldn't know if one was missing. It's possible the Mehlman file was destroyed."

Tommy started to object. Obviously the file wasn't destroyed in the flood. He held the moldy file in his hand. Detective Miller took the papers from Tommy's hand.

"We'll be leaving, then."

Darryl exhaled. "Don't forget your fan."

## 39

DRIVING BACK TO LONG ISLAND, DETECTIVE MILLER opened up to Tommy about the Bayard case. After the job they'd done at Swifty's, the detective believed that Tommy had earned the privilege. He told Tommy about Dr. Bayard and Mr. Gillis, about Hanover Chemical. He even told him a little about chloroform. Tommy was starting to feel like he really was part of the investigation.

Perhaps that explained why, later that evening, he knocked on the door of a freshly painted ranch house in Lynbrook. Mrs. Gillis answered the door in her apron.

"I'm sorry, but if you're selling magazines, I already bought a subscription from the boy next door."

"No, ma'am. I'm not selling magazines. Is your husband home?"

He could hear Mr. Gillis calling from inside the house. "What is it, dear?"

"There's someone here to see you."

When Mr. Gillis got to the front door, he blocked the entrance to discourage any thoughts of the stranger making entry to his home. "Why, you're just a kid."

"Maybe so, but I'm Detective Miller's partner." If Gillis contacted the department, Tommy would be in a heap of trouble, and Detective Miller as well.

"My family is about to sit down to dinner."

Mr. Gillis laughed as he shut the door in Tommy's face. But Tommy managed to get one foot in the door.

Mr. Gillis didn't come back outside and didn't invite Tommy in, but his foot in the door did buy Tommy another chance to engage.

"This will only take a few minutes. It's about the Bayards."

Mrs. Gillis looked at her husband. "Go ahead, dear. I'll keep an eye on the roast."

Mr. Gillis waited until his wife was inside. "I've already told the detective everything I know."

"Yes. I understand that you've been very helpful." Tommy took a quick look at his notepad. The notepad was empty, but effective. "There was gossip at your office about you and Mrs. Bayard."

"Gossip, by its very nature, is unreliable."

Tommy nodded his head in agreement. "That is true, except, of course, when it isn't."

Mr. Gillis tried, unsuccessfully, to hide his irritation. "Let's suppose, speaking hypothetically, that someone was having an affair with Mrs. Bayard. I'm no detective, but I would think that he would be the last person who would want to kill her."

"You may very well be right about that."

Mr. Gillis appeared to relax a bit. "Please tell the detective that he's wasting time on rumors about me and Rosalie. What about the rumors that Dr. Bayard was seeing someone? Wouldn't that be something worth investigating?"

"Yes, it would. Of course, it's also possible that the killer might spread that sort of rumor to divert attention from his own affair with Mrs. Bayard." He scribbled furiously in the notepad, mostly to steady his nerves. "Speaking hypothetically, of course."

"I'm just saying if I was the detective assigned to the case, that's what I'd be investigating."

"You mean instead of interrupting an innocent man's dinner?"

Mr. Gillis didn't bother masking his indignation. "The detective knows that I was bowling the night that Mrs. Bayard was killed. I don't know what you're doing here, but I think you should leave."

"Yes, of course. I'm sorry to have interrupted your dinner." Tommy pretended to check his notes one more time. "By the way, have you heard that the detective identified the man who murdered Mrs. Bayard?"

Mr. Gillis smiled. "Really? That's superb police work. Really first-rate. Please extend my appreciation to the detective. We're fortunate to have such competent detectives here in Nassau County."

"I will. We believe that Mrs. Bayard was murdered by a hitman."

"A mob hit? That doesn't make sense. Why would the mob put out a hit on Mrs. Bayard?"

"The mob didn't. But we're fairly certain someone did. The evidence suggests that someone who worked at Hanover Chemical paid a hitman to kill Mrs. Bayard. Think about it. On the night that she was murdered, the man who paid for the hit could have been anywhere . . . in a restaurant, on a cruise ship, hell, he could have been in a bowling alley. Do you know what that means?"

"I think it means I'm done talking with you."

"As you wish. Enjoy your dinner."

Mr. Gillis slammed the door in Tommy's face.

## 40

SINCE HER MOTHER'S DEATH, EMILY HAD STRUGGLED TO adjust to the emptiness at home. It was more than just the loss of her mother. It was her father's unexpected absence that hurt the most. Emily understood how hard this must be for her father. She understood that he wanted to hide at the office, but just when she needed him the most, he was never home.

Ben was still grounded, waiting for his court date. Emily had no idea where Willow was. There was no one at the ashram when Emily walked in, except Bug. He was cleaning out the walk-in refrigerator. A sign on the wall announced the kitchen was closed by order of the health department.

"What happened?"

Bug pointed to the health department signage. "The health Nazis shut us down."

"I don't understand. You keep the place clean."

"Not clean enough, according to the health department." Bug scowled. "The man can always find an excuse, if he wants to shut you down."

"What are you going to do about it?"

"I've instructed our lawyer to file an appeal."

Emily had never given any thought to the business side of running the ashram. "You have an attorney?"

"Of course we do. Until we change the system, we have to be able to protect our rights in the existing system."

"In the meantime, you're cleaning."

"Yeah."

"All by yourself?"

"Willow and Lily are off at some sort of women's thing. Apparently that's more important to them than the ashram." Bug studied Emily. "I'm surprised you're not with them."

Bug seemed so pitiful, up to his elbows in cleaning solutions, that she stepped in to help.

She cleaned out the grease traps and polished the grill until it shined. She organized the walk-in, tossing anything that even hinted at spoilage. After a couple of hours, she realized that cleaning was a lot like meditating. *Om santih santih santih.*

Bug set aside the array of sponges, mops, and towels. "It was pretty bleak, doing this all by myself."

"I'm sure Willow had a good reason. After all, it's not a frivolous cause."

"What's not frivolous?"

"Equal rights for women. It's important."

"Maybe it is. I'm sure it seems that way to you girls. But it's not as important as black power. It's not as important as ending the war. It's not as important as the ashram."

Emily sighed. "I guess I don't know how to weigh the relative importance of all those things. I just know that women should be treated with respect."

"You're right, of course. Women deserve respect."

Bug bowed from the waist. Emily was reminded of the night they met at Union Station. That seemed so very long ago.

"Women also deserve something to eat after cleaning all day." Bug reached for her. "I would offer to cook something, but as you know, the kitchen is closed."

"I would like to talk to you about your manuscript."

"Come back to the apartment. I'll make dinner." Bug rubbed the knotted muscles in Emily's neck.

She felt lightheaded. Emily told herself it was from breathing in the cleaning products. *Make love, not war*, her hippie friends would say.

"What'll it be?"

"Not tonight." She was grateful that Bug was not a mind reader. She hurried out of the ashram before she could change her mind.

Emily was pleased to see her father's car in the driveway.

Her clothes were filthy, her face smudged, her hair a tangled mess. She needed a hot shower, but first she needed a hug. She ran into the house.

Her father stepped back. "What happened to you?"

"I stopped at the ashram," Emily explained. "It was cleaning day."

"Well, I'm sure a hot shower will do wonders. Go."

"I'm glad you're home."

"Where else would I be?"

"You haven't been home much since Mom died."

"You know . . ." he began, before trailing off.

"Well, you're home now. I'm going to make us dinner. It's time we had a proper Sunday dinner."

"I've got a better idea. How about I order a pizza? By the time you get out of the shower, it should be here."

"Peppers and anchovies?" Emily loved anchovies. Her father, not so much.

"Peppers and anchovies it is."

Thirty minutes later, scrubbed clean, her hair pulled back in a ponytail, Emily settled in with her first slice of pepper and anchovy pizza. Between bites, she thought maybe she could get her father to open up. "I'm worried about you."

"I'm okay."

"No, you're not. All you do anymore is work. Where were you all weekend?"

"At the lab."

"That's exactly what I'm talking about. You can't hide in the lab. At some point, you have to deal with your feelings."

"I'm doing the best I can."

"No, you're not. When you are home, you sleep on the couch. It's like you're afraid to go into your bedroom."

"I'll try to do better."

He turned on the television. Every Sunday at eight, the Bayard family watched Ed Sullivan. Even during the summer, when the shows were repeats, they would watch. Emily sat on the floor right in front of the set.

"It's bad for your eyes."

Ed introduced Patti Page. All year, when Emily got home in the afternoon, her mother would have Patti Page on the Victrola.

Dr. Bayard wiped his face with the back of his hand. Emily got a tissue for her father and another for herself.

After Ed Sullivan, they watched *Bonanza*. Emily had a not-so-secret crush on Little Joe. After *Bonanza*, it was *Mission: Impossible*.

When the news came on, Emily turned off the television. "It's bedtime."

"I'm going to watch the news." He turned the set on.

"I don't want to find you here in the morning, asleep on the sofa."

Emily climbed the stairs and got ready for bed, but not for sleep. From her bedroom, she could hear the television downstairs.

At eleven-thirty, as promised, her father shut off the television. Emily listened for his footsteps on the stairs, but instead, what she heard was the click of the front door. She looked out her window in time to spy her father climbing into his car.

41

BEN WAS TEMPTED TO SCRATCH HASH MARKS INTO THE wall next to his bed, but he didn't want to provoke another confrontation with his father. It had been four days, and he tried to see things from his father's point-of-view. He didn't succeed, but at least he tried. He only wished his father would make the same effort. Maybe he didn't like that Ben had a job at the ashram, but it was a real job, and Ben owed it to Bug to be there.

If the four days were long for Ben, they were an eternity for his mother.

"Are you planning to get dressed sometime today?"

"Today?" Ben stroked his chin, deep in thought. "I don't think so."

"I've had just about enough of this. Go put some clothes on."

"What's the point? Dad says I can't leave the house."

"I can't do this for three more weeks."

"You shouldn't have to." Ben hoped he sounded sympathetic. He needed his mother to be on his side. "Isn't it interesting how Dad grounds me and leaves you here to function as my jailor? It doesn't seem fair."

"Don't you dare talk about your father that way. He's a good man. All he wants is what's best for you."

"All he wants is for me to agree with him."

Like a rain cloud, sadness crossed Mom's face. "He wasn't angry about the speech."

Ben didn't know how to respond. He waited for his mother to continue.

"He was hurt."

"I don't understand."

"You didn't trust him enough to show him the real speech."

"He wouldn't have let me give that speech. Anyway, I didn't know what I was going to say until I said it."

"He didn't agree with what you said, but I know this one thing: he was proud you had the guts to say it."

"But he's always looking for an argument. No matter what I say, Dad disagrees."

"To your father, it feels like you're the one who's always looking for an argument."

"What do you think?"

"I think you're both spoiling for a fight, and I don't understand why."

Ben could tell she'd wanted to say that for weeks.

The Giants were in town for the last time that season. Ben knew things had hit bottom when his father made no plans for the game. As bad as things were, Ben wanted to spend one more night at the ballpark with his father. If he could make that happen, Ben believed his father would let him out of the house.

Ben enlisted his mom's assistance. While Detective Miller was at work, Ben and his mother took the train to Shea Stadium. The box office was open. There were tickets left for the game. Ben couldn't afford good seats, behind the dugout, like his father would have bought, but he could afford the mezzanine level. Ben bought two seats down the right field line.

When his father got home from the station house, Ben asked about the ballgame.

"I didn't think you'd want to go. At least not with your father." He looked at Ben and sighed. "I didn't get tickets."

"But I did." Ben beamed.

His father whistled. "They must pay well at that ashram. Can you afford it?"

"Sure," Ben said, checking his wallet. "As long as you pay for the hot dogs." He checked his wallet one more time. "And the parking."

Detective Miller kissed his wife. "Did you know about this?"

She smiled. It was her first real smile in weeks.

That night, it was hot and humid. Light rain fell intermittently. Detective Miller disappeared during the seventh inning stretch, returning with a bag from the souvenir shop.

"What's this?" Ben asked when his father handed him the bag.

"Open it."

A Mets ballcap. Blue with the orange NY logo.

"Put it on." He laughed. "What? You don't think I knew?"

Ben wore the cap the rest of the game, cheering when the Mets won by the score of 5-3. Tom Seaver got the win.

The baseball wasn't very good. Neither were the seats. The weather was lousy. The traffic on the Cross Island was bumper-to-bumper. They didn't resolve their differences, but for a night, Detective Miller and his son declared a truce, and for the night, at least, the truce held. As they left the ballpark, Detective Miller proclaimed it their best trip ever to Shea Stadium. Ben was inclined to agree.

One night at Shea Stadium was not going to fix everything, but it was a beginning. Ben's mother was smiling more and that took the pressure off both of them. It probably helped that Detective Miller had a small victory at work. A judge granted his request to see Johnny Gee's phone records.

"What do you hope to learn from the phone records?" Ben knew better than to expect an answer and didn't get one.

"I can't talk about official police business."

# 42

BEN WAS ABOUT TO LEAVE THE HOUSE WHEN HE GOT A phone call from Fatty B.

"I saw Emily's father last night. He was at the Sunrise Diner."

"And?"

"He kissed a waitress."

"Are you kidding me?"

Fatty B snorted. "No, man. For real."

"Look, the guy's an asshole, but he's Emily's father." Ben couldn't picture Duncan Bayard messing around with a waitress.

"I know what I saw."

In the car, on the way to the diner, Ben cut to the chase. "So, you think Emily's father is doing it with a waitress."

Fatty was already backing off his story. "Maybe we're jumping to conclusions. All I saw was a kiss."

Ben was beginning to believe the worst. "Not just any kiss. You saw Dr. Bayard, in a diner, after midnight, kissing a waitress."

Fatty B shook his head. "I'm just saying there might be another explanation."

"Do you believe that?"

"It's possible." Fatty turned on the radio. "I don't like the evening guy."

They listened anyway. Anything to block out the image that was stuck in their heads.

"There it is," Ben said, pointing. Fatty pulled the car into the diner's parking lot.

Ben walked into the diner and asked for a booth. Fatty hurried to catch up.

A waitress dropped two menus at the table. "I'll be right back."

She was their parents' age, nothing special to look at, average height, a little chubby, in a pink waitress dress and yellow over-sized eyeglasses.

Ben waited for her to leave. "Is she the one?"

"God, no."

Ben looked around the diner. "Do you see her?"

"I don't think so."

Their waitress reappeared at the booth. "Are you kids ready to order?"

Fatty ordered a short stack of pancakes and coffee.

"Do you want maple syrup with that? We have regular and boysenberry."

"Both."

Ben ordered a turkey club. The waitress returned quickly with the two plates of food.

"That's her," Fatty whispered, trying not to be obvious, a bit of maple syrup dribbling out of the corner of his mouth. "Behind the counter." He picked up his plate and waved to the waitress. "We're changing seats."

Ben grabbed his plate and followed Fatty to the counter. As soon as he sat down, Ben started spinning on the stool.

"You are so immature." But moments later, Fatty did the same thing.

The waitress looked at them like they were crazy. "Do you want a refill?"

Without waiting for an answer, she poured a fresh cup of coffee. Ben decided she had a good enough body, if you went for that type, but he was surprised that Dr. Bayard did—a working girl, with hard edges and a trucker's laugh.

"Thanks."

"If you need anything, just holler. The name's Trixie."

Ben wolfed down the turkey club. Fatty picked at his pancakes.

"Do you kids want anything else?"

"Yes, I do." Ben looked at the waitress, watching for a reaction. "I think you know a friend of ours."

"Is he a regular?"

"His name is Duncan Bayard."

If the waitress knew Emily's father, nothing in her expression gave it away. "I'm sorry, no, I don't recognize the name."

Ben pulled a photograph from his pocket. "Maybe this will help."

Trixie studied the photo. "No, I'm sorry, sweetheart, but I don't recognize him. What's this about, anyway?"

Fatty B stood up, so he could speak to the waitress eye-to-eye. "He came here last night shortly after midnight. You kissed. And then you left together."

"Can I take another look at that photo?" Trixie was stalling.

"Oh, that guy," she finally said, putting down the photo. "He came in here last night, said he'd won a bunch of money in the lottery. Apparently, he bought the winning ticket here. The guy kissed everyone in the diner. It was closing time. I left. He left. Everyone left. End of story."

"That's a load of crap."

"Let me give you a piece of advice, young man."

Ben bristled at her words. "No, let me give you a piece of advice. Stay away from him."

Fatty pulled a couple of dollars out of his wallet. Ben's eyes flashed. "Don't you dare leave that woman a tip."

43

THE KITCHEN AT THE ASHRAM WAS STILL CLOSED, BY ORDER of the health department. Bug was talking to a hippie Ben didn't recognize.

Bug introduced him as Sativa. "I think he can help you."

Ben wasn't sure what Bug was referring to.

Sativa wore blue jeans, a dashiki, and sandals. His hair was pulled back in a ponytail. He flashed a peace sign and handed Ben his business card. Dennis McMichael, Attorney at Law. Licensed in the states of New York and New Jersey.

"Don't worry." Sativa grinned. "I put a suit on when I go to court."

Sativa explained theft of services. "If we go to court, Plan A, you plead guilty, pay a fine, and that's the end of it."

"That doesn't sound too bad." In truth, it sounded like an appropriate punishment for a minor offense, but Ben couldn't shake the feeling that something could still go horribly wrong. He'd been a cop's son a hell of a lot longer than he'd been a hippie.

Bug rolled his eyes.

"What is it?" Willow asked.

"I don't think Ben should pay them a penny."

Sativa examined Ben closely, measuring to see if he was a suitable candidate for Plan B. "There is an alternative."

"I'm listening."

Sativa stood up, as if addressing a jury. "Teenagers sneak into baseball games every day. Does anyone care? No. If an usher catches you, he'll throw you out of his section. But, most of the time, if you're a nice middle-class kid, stadium security looks the other way. For a couple of bucks, they'll direct you to an empty seat. No one gets charged with theft of service at a ballgame."

Sativa was on a roll. "But my client gets arrested for theft of service. Why is that? Is it perhaps because this was a rock and roll show instead of a baseball game? My client is the victim here . . . the victim of blatant discrimination!"

Bug jumped to his feet, applauding. "I told you he was good." Bug turned to Sativa. "What are you suggesting?"

Sativa smiled. "I'm suggesting that Ben file a suit against Shea Stadium and the city of New York for discrimination. I think we can ask for a cool million." He shifted his attention back to Ben. "I don't get anything until we win. Then, I take one-third." Before Ben could do the math, Sativa added, "One-third is standard in a case like this."

"I don't know."

"That's cool. When's your court date?"

"The twenty-seventh."

Sativa checked his calendar. "Don't wait too long to decide. It's going to take me a few days to research the precedents and draw up the papers."

Ben put the business card in his pocket. "Thanks. I'll let you know."

Sativa grabbed Bug by the arm. "How about a pitcher of beer? I'm buying."

Bug looked to Willow.

"Go ahead," she said. "I'm not in the mood."

Bug and Sativa went off in search of cheap beer.

Ben trusted Willow's judgment and needed a second opinion. "What do you think of Sativa's plan?"

"It doesn't matter what I think. You're an adult. What do you think?"

"It sounds a little crazy."

"It sounds more than a little crazy. Have you talked to your father?"

"He thinks I should pay the fine and be happy when it's over."

"That probably makes more sense than filing a lawsuit." Willow paused. "You know, I haven't had a chance to thank you."

"For what?"

"When the matron caught us coming out of the restroom, you gave yourself up. It was sweet of you to do that. You missed a great concert." She leaned in close and kissed Ben.

He picked up the scent of sandalwood. Ben remembered the sandalwood incense in her bedroom. He remembered her purple panties.

"You smell nice."

Willow giggled. "Are you coming on to me?"

Ben didn't know what he was doing.

"It's okay. I like that you're attracted to me." Willow laughed. "And I find it charming that you can't figure out what to do about it."

"I should probably be on my way home."

"Yes. You probably should."

*Om santih santih santih.*

Ben's father had no intention of allowing his son to be represented in court by "one of those long-hairs." Instead, he produced the name of an attorney on Northern Blvd in Jackson Heights and made an appointment for Wednesday morning.

They sat in the waiting room for nearly an hour before a secretary took them into a conference room. The room was paneled in blond wood. The conference table matched the paneling. Ten chocolate-colored leather chairs surrounded the table. One chair was significantly larger than the others. There was no doubt who the oversized chair belonged to.

Mr. Cavendish was tall, thin, and dressed in an expensive European suit. Cuff links flashed at his wrist. He had a firm handshake. He was not an especially large man, but when Mr. Cavendish sat, he filled the oversized chair.

"Gentlemen, I'm sorry to keep you waiting. Please sit down. How can I help you?"

Detective Miller spoke first. "My son got himself into a bit of trouble. He has a court appearance on the twenty-seventh."

There were two yellow legal pads on the conference table. Mr. Cavendish jotted down the court date. He pushed the second legal pad across the table and smiled warmly. "In case you want to take notes."

"Thank you." Detective Miller resumed his narrative. "As I was saying—"

Mr. Cavendish interrupted him. "If it's okay with you, I'd like to hear the details directly from your son."

Ben told Mr. Cavendish all about the Festival for Peace. He told him about the counterfeit tickets. The chain link fence along the bullpen. The ladies' room, the matron, and the mustard. Mr. Cavendish took notes. Detective Miller did, too. With all those notes, Ben chose his words with care.

Mr. Cavendish allowed Ben to tell the entire story without interruption. Ben liked that. Adults were always interrupting.

When Ben finished, Mr. Cavendish made a final note on his pad. "I've had a chance to do my homework. Evidently, there were people in the Borough President's Office as well as in the Shea Stadium hierarchy who had misgivings about the Festival. Between Woodstock and the recent student demonstrations, there was a feeling that things might get out of control."

Mr. Cavendish turned his attention to Ben's father. "You're a detective, am I right?"

"Fifth Precinct. Nassau County."

"So, you understand what happens in situations like that."

"I believe the cops were told to enforce everything, no matter how minor. No exceptions. No discretion."

"That's right. Fortunately, the Festival was a success. All the court wants now is to process a couple dozen misdemeanors without clogging up the system or creating any bad press. I'm confident we can come to a pre-trial settlement."

"That sounds good."

Mr. Cavendish turned to Ben. "What about you, Ben? Does it sound good to you?"

"I think so, sir. Yes, it does." Ben smiled. "It sounds very good."

"Okay, then. With your permission, I'll reach out to the DA. I'd like to wrap this up quickly."

Mr. Cavendish pulled a sheaf of papers from his case and explained his hourly rates. Ben and his father both signed the paperwork and with that completed, said their goodbyes.

"You seem like a good kid. Don't worry. I'll make sure everything comes out okay." Mr. Cavendish smiled warmly. "If we have to make a court appearance, you might want to trim your hair a little bit."

They felt pretty good after their appointment with Mr. Cavendish. On the way home, Ben thought he might even get his father to share some information about Emily's mother. At a red light, he cleared his throat and gave it a try.

"How are you doing with the Bayard case? Are you close to making an arrest?"

"You know I can't talk to you about an open case."

"I know. So, anyway, is it true that Dr. Bayard is a suspect?"

Detective Miller stared at the traffic light. "Who told you that?"

"People."

"People talk too much."

"Yes, they do. The thing is, Emily hears all of it. Do you know how hard that is for her? Do you know how hard it is for me?"

The light turned green. "I'm sorry, son, but there's nothing I can tell you."

# 44

IF HIS FATHER WASN'T GOING TO TELL HIM WHAT WAS going on, Ben would have to figure it out on his own. He owed that much to Emily.

It was dinner time when he pulled into the diner's parking lot. The Sunrise Diner was packed.

A middle-aged woman stood behind the cash register. "Good evening, officer. I'll have a table available in a couple of minutes."

Ben didn't look like a seasoned detective, but, in his father's old uniform, he could pass for a rookie cop. "That won't be necessary." He flashed an ID. He was counting on the woman not looking at anything too closely. "I'm here to speak to one of your waitresses. I believe her name is Trixie."

The woman gasped. "Is she in trouble? I don't need trouble in my diner."

"No. I just need to ask her a few questions."

"I'm sorry. Trixie is off today. If you give me a moment, I'll check her schedule for the rest of the week."

"That won't be necessary. But if you can give me her address, that would be helpful. I'll talk to her at home. That way, I don't need to interrupt her while she's working."

"Thank you, yes. I'd appreciate that. I just need a moment." The hostess pulled a composition book out of a drawer below the counter and flipped through the pages. "Ah, there it is."

Ben copied the address into his notepad. "Thank you."

"You're quite welcome. We're always happy to assist the boys in blue. Come back when you have time to eat. It's on the house."

It was late by the time he knocked on the door of Trixie's garden apartment. If she recognized him from his visit to the diner, he would be in a mess of trouble. It was a gamble, but he was counting on the police uniform to get by.

"Excuse me, are you Trixie?"

"Who wants to know?"

He flashed the ID and mumbled, "Miller, Fifth Precinct."

"Please come in. Don't mind the mess." A Murphy bed was up against the wall, laundry draped over two folding chairs. "Can I offer you a drink?"

"No, thank you, ma'am. I'm on duty."

"Of course you are. So, what can I do for you?"

Ben pulled a photo from his pocket. "Do you know this man?"

"Sure. That's Duncan."

"How do you know Duncan?"

Trixie told Ben about the first time he came into the diner. "He had a fight with his wife. She locked him out."

"You're sure about that?"

"Yeah. I'm usually off on Friday, but I was covering for a friend. Duncan came in to use the phone. He told me his wife had locked him out."

"Is that all?"

"He was cute. I told him if he needed a place to sleep, he could sleep with me." Trixie laughed. "I guess that makes me sound kind of slutty, huh?"

"It's not my place to judge, ma'am. Is that the only time you slept with Dr. Bayard?"

Trixie's eyes lit up. "I didn't know he was a doctor."

"A chemist. Anyway, is that the only time you saw him?"

"Two nights later, he showed up at the diner at closing time."

"I take it he wasn't there for a meal?"

"Like I said, it was closing time." Trixie blushed. "Look, I'm glad to help out, but I'm meeting my girlfriend at a club tonight. Are you finished?"

"Almost." Again Ben checked the notepad. "And you're certain that he told you his wife had locked him out?"

"Absolutely!"

"So, you would be surprised if I told you that his wife was murdered, nearly two months ago?"

"Holy shit, yes!" Trixie connected the dots. "He lied to me. Why do I always end up with the assholes?" She shook her head in disgust. "If she was already dead, how did she lock him out? That doesn't seem possible."

"I would say it was highly improbable."

"Did he kill his wife?"

"I don't know, ma'am. That's why we investigate."

"But you think he might have? Am I in any danger?"

"I don't believe there's any particular threat. But sleeping with strangers is always dangerous. Under the circumstances, I'd advise caution."

## 45

ARTIE SPENT HIS DAYS PULLING LOBSTER TRAPS AND HIS evenings walking with Mary. He was making slow progress learning how to spot the constellations. Mary tried to show him the Summer Triangle.

"The Summer Triangle is easy."

"Maybe for you, but not for me."

As they walked, they shared small intimacies. They discussed books and movies. They walked past the Breakwater Cinema.

Mary smiled shyly. "Do you like jujubes?"

"I guess so."

"I'm glad. I could never go to the movie theater with a man who doesn't like jujubes."

Artie brightened at the idea of going to the movies with Mary.

But the movies would have to wait. They continued walking, arriving, as they did each night, in front of the Red Sky Convalescent Hospital. Artie pulled a cigarette out of the pack, prepared to wait for Mary on the porch.

"Why don't you come inside? I'd like you to meet my mother."

"Your mother?"

They walked into the lobby, stopping at the front desk to sign the guest book. Mary greeted the woman at the reception desk and introduced her to Artie.

Red Sky called itself a hospital, but it didn't look like one to Artie.

Mary led him down the hall to her mother's room. There were trees painted on the walls. The ceiling looked like a summer sky. It was a nice enough place. Or would be, Artie decided, if not for the wheelchairs and gurneys lined up alongside the nurses' station.

Mary's mother's room was just beyond the nurses' station. Artie hung back, lingering outside the door.

"Come on in. I want to introduce you." Mary turned to the frail woman, all skin and bones, lying in bed. "Mom, this is Artie. He's the boy I told you about. Artie, this is Mom. She likes to be called Ida."

The woman looked at Artie, but her thoughts were somewhere else. Her eyes blinked furiously. Her hands trembled. Her thin body was stiff. "Are you here to take me to the dance?"

Artie didn't know how to answer.

"Cat got your tongue?" When Ida spoke, it sounded like her tongue was too big for her mouth. "That's okay. I like shy boys." She laughed, a dry laugh, more cough than laugh.

"No," said Mary. "This is my friend, Artie. Do you remember? I told you about Artie."

Mary chatted with her mother. She talked about the boarding home. She told her mother about her vegetable garden. She discussed current events.

"Who's taking me to the dance?" Ida began shaking her fists and shouting. "Who's taking me to the dance?" She pulled at the bedding, twisting it in her hands. A nurse came on the run, exchanging looks with Mary. No words were needed. The nurse gave Ida a shot.

Ida stopped shaking her fists. She mumbled, "Who's taking me to the dance?" and then fell silent.

Mary resumed their conversation as though nothing had happened. "President Nixon signed a bill to reform the post office. I think that's probably a good idea. What do you think?"

But her mother wasn't listening. She had no interest in current events, or any events, for that matter.

Artie wasn't listening either. He stared at an oversized corkboard attached to the far wall. Hundreds of photos, eerily familiar, all of them pictures of Mary.

Mary gave her mother a kiss and said goodnight. They said goodbye to the night nurse and hurried back to the boarding home.

It was not a night for astronomy. The constellations were hidden behind a blanket of clouds. It didn't really matter. Neither of them was in the mood for constellations.

## 46

ARTIE WAS PUTTING ON A YELLOW RAIN SLICKER, PREPAR-
ing for a rainy morning on the lobster boat, when Mary
approached.

"I hoped it would go better."

"Is she always like that?"

Mary didn't answer right away. "It wasn't so bad at the start,
but it's been getting worse."

Artie didn't want to overstep any boundaries. "If you don't
mind my asking, what is the matter with her?"

"My mother suffers from Parkinson's disease."

"I don't know what that is."

"I didn't either until she got the diagnosis."

"So, that place, Red Sky, she's getting treatment there, right?
She'll get better."

"No, she won't get better. She'll only get worse."

Artie was puzzled. "Why can't they do more for your mother?
What if we took her to New York to see a specialist?"

"It's complicated." She looked at her wristwatch. "Go. The lobsters won't wait forever." Mary turned to Joe for help.

"C'mon, Artie. The rain is only going to get worse."

It was a wet, dreary day on the lobster boat. Artie went
through the motions, pulling up the lobster traps, collecting the

day's crustaceans. Something about the way the lobsters shook their claws reminded him of Ida. Artie reached for a pot and missed.

Joe was at the helm. "Your mind's not on lobstering."

"I'm thinking about Mary's mother."

"It's a sad case."

"Mary said she'll keep getting worse. Isn't there something the doctors can do?"

"I don't think so. At least she has Red Sky. According to Mary, there are only a couple of places like it. She's fortunate to find one in Breakwater."

Artie pulled a string of traps. "What is Red Sky, anyway? The sign says it's a hospital, but it sure doesn't look like one."

Joe shrugged. "What do I know? I dropped out of school in the middle of eighth grade. If you want a better answer, talk to Mary."

Two days went by before Artie had an opportunity to ask Mary about Red Sky. Sunday, after church, sipping iced tea, he asked.

"What did you mean when you said your mother won't get better?"

"I meant she's dying." Mary wiped her face with a towel that she kept at her waist. "That's why she's at Red Sky."

"Yeah, that too. I don't understand."

Mary smiled. "When she was in the regular hospital, the doctors did everything they were supposed to do, only nothing worked."

"I'm sorry."

"Don't apologize. It's not your fault. Not the doctors' either. But we reached a point where the only thing the hospital could do was to prolong her agony. I don't want that for my mother. Red Sky will allow her to die with dignity."

"So, is everyone at Red Sky dying?"

"Most of the patients die within a few weeks of transferring from the hospital."

"What about your mother?"

Mary didn't know whether to laugh or cry. "She's been at Red Sky for five months."

"So, that's good, isn't it?" Artie could tell from Mary's face that it was not a good thing, not a good thing at all. He remembered a conversation, that first evening when they went for a walk. "I'm so sorry."

After dinner, Joe volunteered to wash the dishes. Artie invited Mary to join him at the Breakwater Cinema.

"Did you arrange this with Joe?"

When they got to the cinema, they bought jujubes and buttered popcorn and had their pick of seats in the nearly empty theater. They watched the coming attractions and the feature film and tried not to think about death and dying. Artie considered putting his arm around Mary's shoulders, but he didn't think she'd approve of such a public display of affection.

On the way home, they stopped at the five and dime. They sat at the counter and talked while drinking cherry colas. Artie browsed through a rack of greeting cards. He bought a birthday card and a postage stamp and slipped the card, unsigned, in the curbside mailbox. He didn't offer an explanation, and Mary didn't ask.

## 47

WHEN DR. BAYARD ARRIVED AT WORK, THE LAB WAS HALF-empty. He had forgotten about the outing. Every year, on a warm summer day, Hanover Chemical would hold a company outing. They promoted it as a team-building event, but in truth, it was an excuse for the company decision-makers to play a round of golf on company time.

Dr. Bayard was not a golfer, but he recognized that golf was part of the career ladder at Hanover. It wasn't enough to know the difference between dialuminum selenide and dialuminum telluride. If he didn't know the difference between a sand wedge and a pitching wedge, he would not have a future at Hanover. He bought a set of clubs and asked one of the senior executives for the name of a local pro. He took lessons until he could play well enough to avoid making a fool of himself. He would play from time to time, if he couldn't come up with an excuse.

This time he had an excellent excuse. His meeting in Washington was less than two weeks away, and there were still issues to be resolved in the lab.

With most of his team on the golf course, Dr. Bayard had the chance to do actual chemistry rather than manage a team of chemists. The day passed quickly, Dr. Bayard alone in the lab, running tests.

It was late in the afternoon when Karen called.

"We missed you today on the golf course."

"We?"

"Well, I missed you. When you're finished at the lab, why don't you come to my house? I'll make us dinner and after dinner, we'll see what happens."

Dr. Bayard knew what "we'll see" meant. It meant, perhaps this time, he would be able to satisfy his girlfriend.

Dr. Bayard's biggest problem on the golf course was visualization. The pro wanted him to visualize hitting the ball long and straight, landing it in the middle of the fairway. But when he stood on the tee and prepared to hit the ball, he imagined hitting a duck hook, landing the ball in the woods, or in a water hazard. Worse yet, he imagined dribbling the ball off the tee or missing it completely. Dr. Bayard realized that sex was a lot like golf.

"I'm making Italian food. Can you stop on the way over and pick up a bottle of wine?"

"Of course."

"I love you, Duncan."

"And I love you, Karen."

When he got to her house, the evening went exactly as Dr. Bayard expected. Karen served a candlelight dinner of veal parmesan and spaghetti. They finished the bottle of Chianti. When Karen suggested that they go to bed, it was like he was standing on the first tee. Visualization. Karen reached into his golf bag. She tried to hide her disappointment. "Maybe it's time you talked to somebody."

"You mean, like a therapist? I'm supposed to tell a therapist how, ever since my wife died, I can't get it up for my girlfriend? No thank you. That's not a conversation I want to have."

"Well, you need to do something."

"You're right." Duncan climbed out of bed, put on his clothes, said goodbye, and drove to Trixie's.

# 48

IT WAS AFTER MIDNIGHT WHEN DR. BAYARD PARKED HIS car in the lot alongside Trixie's garden apartment. She would be home soon enough. He sat in the car, reading the newspaper. Lieutenant Calley's court martial had been postponed. The Vatican restored diplomatic relations with Yugoslavia. The Army and the state of Florida were in court arguing about the disposal of nerve gas. And the FDA was banning the use of cyclamates.

Dr. Bayard made a note to raise the last item with senior management. The deforestation project was working its way to a conclusion. Whether it resulted in a contract or not, when the research was finished, Dr. Bayard would need to find a new project. Perhaps it was time to look into artificial sweeteners.

It was nearly three in the morning when Trixie's car pulled into the parking lot. She bumped the curb as she pulled into her spot. She was dressed in a yellow mini-skirt and purple go-go boots. Duncan climbed out of his car and intercepted Trixie before she could go inside.

"Where have you been?"

"I've been out clubbing." Trixie frowned. "Not that it's any of your business."

Dr. Bayard smelled of red wine, cigarettes, and desperation. "I've been waiting for you."

"That's not my problem."

"I'm sorry. It's just, I had a rough night; I could use a little loving."

"More trouble with the wifey?"

"That woman is making me crazy. So, anyway, can I come in?"

"Not tonight. I'm tired and I have a headache."

Dr. Bayard grabbed her wrist. "Which is it? Are you tired or do you have a headache?"

Trixie winced. "Hey, that hurts. Let go of me, Duncan."

"Why don't we go inside and have some fun?" He tightened his grip. "You know you want to."

"Let go of me right now, or I swear I'm going to call the police."

"How dare you!" Dr. Bayard raised his free hand as if to strike her.

"Don't," screamed Trixie. "Just don't."

A window opened in a second-floor apartment. "Is everything okay down there?"

"Go back to sleep. Everything's fine."

"Then do us all a favor and shut the fuck up." The window closed.

Dr. Bayard released his grip on Trixie's wrist. "I'm sorry. It's been a really bad day."

"The next time you have a bad day, keep it to yourself. I've got better things to do." Trixie walked to the apartment door. "In fact, just stay away from me. We're finished, Duncan."

"What do you mean, we're finished? I thought we were having fun."

"Fun only goes so far. After a while a girl needs more than fun."

"Tell me, Trixie. What do you need? Whatever it is, I can get it for you."

"What I need is a man who's not a person of interest in a police investigation. Can you get that for me?"

Trixie slammed the door without waiting for an answer. "Goodnight."

## 49

TOMMY CALLAHAN HAD TAKEN TO HANGING OUT WITH Detective Miller. Mornings at Sonny's and afternoons at the Fifth. Detective Miller was surprisingly calm, considering the reaming the Captain had given him about Tommy's unauthorized visit to the Gillis home.

"Just don't do it again," the detective told Tommy. "In fact, don't do anything without my knowledge and approval. Is that clear?"

Before Tommy could answer, Detective Miller got a phone call.

"This is Detective Miller."

Trixie had slept poorly. Her wrist was bruised and sore. She winced when she squeezed the tube of toothpaste. It hurt when she dialed the phone. "It's Trixie Pilson. When I got home last night, he was waiting for me."

"I'm sorry, Miss Pilson, is it?" Detective Miller didn't recognize the name or the voice. He glanced at Tommy, asking without words if this was his doing. Tommy shook his head no. Emphatically no.

"I'm afraid you have me at a disadvantage."

"You came to my apartment. You asked me about Dr. Bayard."

Detective Miller hadn't been to her apartment. And he hadn't questioned her about Dr. Bayard. He was at a loss to explain why Miss Pilson believed that he had. But it was evident that she knew something about Dr. Bayard that he didn't. He was happy to play along.

"So, it was Dr. Bayard who was waiting for you?"

"I got home late. He was sitting in his car, outside my apartment."

"What did he want?"

"What do you think he wanted?" Trixie snorted. "He wanted sex. I said no."

"Good. Did he do anything?"

"The bastard grabbed me. My wrist is black and blue. It hurts when I try to pour a glass of orange juice. It hurts when I try to brush my teeth."

"So, he assaulted you. Did you file a complaint?"

"He didn't assault me. Aren't you listening, Detective? I said he grabbed my wrist."

"Do you want to file a complaint?"

"No. I don't want to file a complaint. Look, Detective, I don't want to get involved, but I figured you should know. I mean, since you're already investigating him for murder."

Grabbing a woman by the wrist was wrong, but it wasn't generally a matter for the police. And yet, somehow, this woman was connected to the murder investigation. Detective Miller briefed the Captain and decided to pick up Dr. Bayard for questioning. Given his recent misstep with Mr. Gillis, he should have left Tommy behind, but Detective Miller decided to bring him along.

In the car, the detective finished lecturing Tommy about his visit to the Gillis home. "If you're going to be a cop, you can't let an honest mistake derail an investigation."

"But what if Mr. Gillis sees me at Hanover?"

"Then he sees you." Detective Miller paused to curse at a car driving too slowly in the fast lane. "Just do your job."

"What is my job?"

"Keep your mouth shut and your eyes open."

When they arrived at Hanover Chemical, Detective Miller flashed his badge at the security guard and kept walking. He didn't slow down until he arrived at the upstairs reception area. Tommy hurried to keep up.

"I'm sorry, Detective. Dr. Bayard is in a meeting."

He nodded at Karen and opened the door to Bayard's office. Dr. Bayard was drinking a cup of coffee and reading the morning paper.

"How dare you! This is a private office!"

Detective Miller scowled. Tommy said nothing and watched.

"Tell you what, let's have this conversation down at my private office."

"I'm not talking to you any more without my attorney."

"That's fine. Tell him to meet us at the Fifth Precinct."

"But I have important work to do. I don't have time for this today."

"That's okay. You might want to tell your secretary to clear your calendar."

"Am I under arrest?"

"Not yet."

Karen Conaway stared as Dr. Bayard came out of his office and left with the detective without saying a word.

"I've already told you everything I know about Rosalie."

The detective looked at Bayard in the rearview mirror. "This isn't about Rosalie."

Dr. Bayard was sweating in the hot car. "What else could it be about?"

"The waitress at the Sunrise Diner."

"That bitch! What did she say?"

"You went to see her last night."

Dr. Bayard started to answer and then thought better of it. "I really should wait for my attorney."

"As you wish."

# 50

WHEN THEY ARRIVED AT THE FIFTH PRECINCT, DETECTIVE
Miller put Dr. Bayard in an interrogation room. "You can wait
here until your attorney arrives."

It was midafternoon when Mr. Davenport walked into the station house looking for Dr. Bayard. Tommy escorted the attorney
to Detective Miller's desk. The detective took him to the interrogation room.

Bayard scowled at the lawyer. "It's about time."

"I had a busy day." Mr. Davenport adopted a pained expression.
"You do understand that I'm not a criminal attorney. I do patent law."

Mr. Davenport took a seat next to his client. Detective Miller
sat down across the table and began the interview. Tommy
watched through the one-way mirror.

"How would you characterize your relationship with Trixie
Pilson?"

"I know her, if that's what you mean."

"I mean, are you sleeping with her?"

Davenport put his hand on Bayard's arm. "You don't have to
answer that."

"It's none of your business whether I've slept with her. There's
nothing illegal about a man and a woman spending the night
together."

"No, there isn't. But in my experience, it is unusual for a man to have sex with a woman when his wife has just recently been murdered."

"I advise you not to answer."

Bayard laughed nervously. "He didn't ask a question."

"Here's a question. Where were you this morning at three?"

"It seems you already know, Detective. Why don't you tell me?"

"You were in Miss Pilson's parking lot."

"Maybe I was. I don't see why that's of interest to the police."

"You approached Miss Pilson. The two of you argued. You assaulted her."

"That's a lie!" He jumped out of his seat, screaming. "I did not assault that woman!"

"Sit down, Bayard. You grabbed her with enough force that her wrist is bruised. That qualifies as assault."

The Captain opened the door to the interrogation room. "There's a phone call for you, Detective."

Miller knew the Captain wouldn't interrupt the interrogation unless it was important. He looked at Bayard and Davenport. "Wait here."

When they were in the hallway, the Captain explained. "You've got a call from Assistant Superintendent Shephard at Clinton Correctional."

Detective Miller hurried to his desk and grabbed the phone. Tommy hurried after the detective, fully prepared to say nothing and watch. For Tommy's benefit, Detective Miller put the call on speakerphone.

"How are things in Dannemora?"

"It's Senior's birthday."

"Damn. If I knew, I would have sent him a present."

"That's okay. He got a birthday card in the mail."

"From Junior?"

"The card was unsigned, with no return address, but who else would send the old man an unsigned birthday card?"

"You're right. It's from Junior. Anything else?"

"The envelope was postmarked in Breakwater, Maine. I know it's not much, but I figured it might mean something."

"Thanks. It's a start."

Miller hung up the phone and returned to the interrogation room. Tommy returned to his spot at the one-way mirror. "Sorry for the interruption. It appears we just identified the whereabouts of Johnny Gee Junior. You remember Junior, don't you?"

"I don't—"

"Don't say anything, Duncan." Mr. Davenport looked to Detective Miller for clarification of his client's status. "Is my client under arrest?"

"No, not yet."

"Then we're done here." Mr. Davenport paused. "I can do that, right?"

The detective nodded. "You can do that."

Mr. Davenport stood up. "Come on, Duncan. We're leaving."

"A word of advice before you go. This department does not take kindly to violence against women. It is only a matter of time before I have Junior. Next time we do this, you won't be able to get up and leave."

"Is that a threat, Detective?"

"Be quiet, Duncan!" Mr. Davenport tugged at Bayard's arm. "We're leaving."

"You should listen to your attorney."

"I'll have your badge. Nobody threatens Duncan Bayard. Nobody!"

"My client is distraught. He doesn't know what he's saying." Mr. Davenport pulled Dr. Bayard out of the interrogation room.

Detective Miller watched the two men walk down the hall, arguing.

It was only a matter of time.

# 51

DETECTIVE MILLER LOCATED AN ATLAS IN THE STATION
house and stared at the map of Maine. Apparently, Breakwater
was on the coast. He placed a phone call to the police department.

"Good afternoon, this is Officer Hilliard. How can I direct your
call?"

"Hello, Officer. This is Detective Stanley Miller. I'm calling
from the Nassau County Police Department. I'm investigating a
murder down here in New York, and I think my suspect may be
in Breakwater."

"Hoo boy. That's not a call we get every day."

"Anyway, I guess you can connect me to one of your detectives."

Officer Hilliard chuckled. "Excuse my sense of humor. I'm
the only one in the station this afternoon. But if you give me the
information, I'll see what I can do."

"I'm looking for Johnny Gee Junior, but it's more likely you'd
know him as Artie Mehlman. Do either of those names mean
anything to you?"

"I'm afraid not. If you don't mind my asking, why do you think
he's in Breakwater?"

"Evidence suggests that he mailed a letter from the Breakwater
Post Office a couple of days ago."

"It's possible he was just passing through town. There's not much reason for a stranger to be here in Breakwater."

"Would it be easy for a stranger to avoid notice in Breakwater?"

"We're a small town, Detective, but we believe that people have a right to privacy. We don't pry without a compelling reason."

"I would think that murder would be a compelling reason."

"I'll talk to the sergeant."

"Thank you. I'll send you a photo."

"I spend most of my time settling arguments between fishermen. It'd be pretty neat to be able to tell my wife that I helped solve a New York murder."

"If you help me find Junior, that's exactly what you can tell her. Your sergeant, too."

"I'll try my best, Detective."

"I'm counting on it, Officer."

# 52

ARTIE WAS ON HIS WAY TO THE LOBSTER BOAT WHEN JOE made a surprising announcement.

"I have a family emergency in Boston. I'll be gone for a couple of days."

"When are you leaving?"

"Tonight."

"Is there anything I can do to help?"

Joe had an answer at the ready. "You can run the business until I get back."

Artie put up his hands to bring Joe to a halt. "I can't do that. I can't hardly run the boat, let alone the business."

Joe ignored Artie's objection. "You know how to set the traps and how to haul them. You know how to handle the boat. You'll be fine."

Artie shook his head vehemently. "I won't be fine. I don't know what I'm doing."

"I can't afford to let the boat sit at the dock while I'm gone. I'm still paying off the new engine. I've been watching you, Artie. You can do this."

"Of course I can do it when you're watching. If I screw up, I know you'll be there to fix things."

"You're not going to screw up. Think of today like a practice run. You'll see. It's going to be okay."

Artie cast off the lines and nudged the boat away from the dock at idle speed. He felt like a teenager, taking his father's car out for a spin for the first time. That hadn't ended so well, either.

Gripping the wheel tight, he scanned for hazards and brought the boat out into open water. As he approached the first string of traps, Artie idled the engine, leaned out to the side, and snagged the line. Thankfully, the weather was good, the water calm, and the lobster plentiful.

Still, he found the solo routine nerve-wracking. It didn't get easier, but he did manage to get through the day without any major mishaps.

On the way back into the harbor, Artie slowed the boat to a crawl and steered for the dock, remembering how Joe did it. He bumped the dock with the boat's bow, but not so hard as to cause any damage. Finally, he cut the engine and secured the lines.

Joe was impressed but didn't let on. "We're not done yet. You still have to sell the lobsters."

Artie had been wondering about that all day. Joe didn't ever talk about the business end of the lobster business. Artie knew that Joe sold his lobsters to a wholesaler, but he wasn't privy to the details.

"I've been dealing with the same wholesaler for a couple of years now. Come on. I'll introduce you."

Joe located his wholesaler and made the introductions. They offloaded the lobsters and weighed them. It was a simple cash transaction.

"That's not so hard, now is it?"

"Not unless something goes wrong."

"I'm only going to be gone for a few days. I'll ask a couple of the other lobstermen to keep an eye on you. If you get into any serious trouble, the Coast Guard will come get you."

Artie's first day alone on the water was uneventful. He walked back to the boarding home with a sizable roll of bills in his pocket and fell asleep before dinner was served. He was looking forward to another day alone on the water.

The second day started off just like the first. Then Artie spotted a lobsterman hauling a few of Joe's traps. He knew they were Joe's by the orange markings. Artie yelled, but the lobster thief ignored him. Artie had been told that such things rarely happened and when they did, they were settled with fisticuffs.

There wasn't much Artie could do while he was out on the water. He finished up the day's work without making things any worse, but his load was light. The wholesaler noticed the difference.

"Not as good as yesterday."

Artie didn't know whether he was supposed to say something. He decided to put his trust in Joe's wholesaler. "Someone poached Joe's lobsters."

The wholesaler pointed to a boat making its way into the harbor. "Is that him?"

Artie checked him out. An older man, wiry and mean-looking. "Yeah, that's him."

"That's Milo. You're not the first guy to have a problem with Milo."

"So, what am I supposed to do?"

"Most of the lobstermen, if they don't have anything better to do, head to Blackbeard's for a whiskey. If you want to make Milo stop, you need to confront him, in Blackbeard's in front of everyone."

"I'm not looking for trouble."

"It doesn't matter. Trouble is looking for you."

Since coming to Breakwater, Artie had kept a low profile. With the exception of four people at the boarding home, a couple of night nurses at Red Sky and the wholesaler, no one knew he existed. Artie liked it that way. He didn't relish the idea of a public confrontation. Still, he owed it to Joe to do something.

Artie made his way to Blackbeard's, stepped up to the bar, and ordered a shot of rye and a beer chaser. The bar was packed with lobstermen and their hard-earned cash and the women who were determined to separate them from that cash. He knocked down the shot and ordered another.

After the second, he was ready to confront Milo. Artie stood up with every intention of challenging Milo to the lobsterman's equivalent of a duel.

Much to Artie's surprise, another lobsterman beat him to it. As the wholesaler had told him, Artie wasn't the only one to have a problem with Milo.

Milo threw the first punch. Artie was grateful another man's face was the target. It didn't take long for the fight to spread and for a police car to pull up to the bar, sirens blasting.

No benefit would come to Artie if he were sucked into the melee. After a day on the lobster boat, two shots of rye had turned his legs to rubber. He stumbled but made his way out the rear exit as a police officer entered through the front.

It was past dinnertime, but Mary kept a plate warming in the kitchen. Standing at the kitchen counter, Artie polished off two pieces of fried chicken, wax beans, and a baked potato with sour cream.

Mary kept him company as he ate. "How was your day?"

She didn't need to know about Milo. "It was good." Artie looked at Mary and smiled. "I'll be happy when Joe gets back." He sipped the iced tea.

Mary didn't press for an explanation. "Can you walk with me tonight?"

"Of course." His exhaustion was a distant memory. "Just give me a moment to clean myself up."

"I think you're fine just the way you are."

Artie knew it wasn't true, but he liked that she said so. "Only if you like the smell of engine grease and lobster shells."

He excused himself, returning a few minutes later wearing a clean shirt. The smell of grease and crustacean was more subtle, mingled with the hearty scent of Old Spice.

They walked into town, taking their time, holding hands. Artie offered to buy a fountain soda, but Mary declined. "Let's just walk."

It was getting late. "We should go say goodnight to your mother."

Mary sighed. "Yes. Of course."

When they got to Red Sky, one of the patients was on the porch, pacing. Mary recognized the elderly gentleman.

"Are you okay?" she asked.

"It's noisy in there."

They could hear screaming coming from the far end of the hallway. Mary knew immediately that it was Ida. Without stopping to sign the visitor's log, she hurried down the hall.

A nurse and two orderlies were in Ida's room.

"I gave her a shot," the nurse said. "She should settle down."

Mary looked at her mother. "Hello, Ida."

Ida stopped screaming. "Hello, dear. It's so nice of you to come for a visit. My name's Ida. What's yours?"

Before Mary could answer, Ida closed her eyes. Mary pulled a chair up next to the bed, sat down, and stroked the back of her mother's hand. Artie leaned against the wall and waited.

Thirty minutes later, the nurse peeked into the room. Mary was still sitting in the chair, Artie was still leaning against the wall, and Ida was still sleeping, or pretending to.

"If you need anything, just ask. My name's Phyllis. I'm new here."

Mary looked up. "Thank you, Phyllis. I'm her daughter . . . Mary."

"I figured you were. The chart says you come by and say goodnight nearly every night."

"Every night that I can."

"I think that's sweet. Does your mother like it here?"

"I don't know." Mary considered the question. "I don't think she knows where here is."

"Well, anyway, remember, if you need anything, I'm here to help." With that, Phyllis departed, down the hall to other patients and other problems.

Mary stood up slowly, unkinking the muscles in her back. "I think it's time for us to go."

They left the room together and walked down the hall, stopping at the reception desk.

The receptionist smiled. "How is your mother?"

"The same as always, I guess. I really don't know any more."

"You're a good daughter."

"That's better," Mary said when they stepped out into the cool night air, inhaling and exhaling deeply. "I couldn't breathe." She kissed Artie on the cheek. "Thanks for coming with me."

On the way back to the boarding home, they stopped to look at the stars. For the first time, Artie located the Summer Triangle.

"You're getting the hang of it." Mary smiled. "My mother's name is Claudia."

"I thought it was Ida."

"When she transferred to Red Sky, during the intake interview, she told a social worker her name was Ida. It's been Ida ever since."

Mary kissed him again. It was an uncommon kiss, in Artie's experience, the sort of kiss that came from someplace deep in the soul, the sort of kiss that came with a promise.

## 53

ARTIE WAS SITTING ON THE PORCH, SMOKING A CHESTER-field, when Mary stepped outside. She hardly noticed him sitting there as she headed down the steps to the street.

"Do you want company?"

Mary jumped at the sound of his voice. "I think I need to be alone tonight."

"Is everything okay?"

"Sort of," she said. Mary tried to explain. "This is something I have to do all by myself."

"Sometimes, the best way to be alone is with someone else."

"Not tonight." She kissed him quickly. "Be here when I get back?"

"Of course."

"I won't be long." With that, Mary walked off.

It wasn't Artie's intention to follow her, not exactly. It just worked out that way.

Of course, it helped that he knew where she was going.

Artie felt foolish, standing on the sidewalk in front of Red Sky. He worried that Mary would be mad at him. She had been clear in her desire to be left alone. He retreated deeper into the darkness.

Suddenly Mary came bursting out of Red Sky, tears streaming down her face. Artie didn't have time to worry about making her angry. He stepped out of the darkness. Mary folded herself in his arms and cried.

She couldn't stop crying, but Artie could see it in her eyes. She was glad to find him waiting there. She grabbed his hand and pulled him down the street.

"What's wrong, Mary?"

"Not here." She continued to drag Artie down the street, tears rolling down her face. She dragged him all the way to the harbor, where she finally came to a stop, out-of-breath and panting.

"What's the matter?"

She pulled out a tissue and blew her nose. She pulled out another tissue and wiped her eyes. She pointed toward the sky. "Cassiopeia."

"What happened at Red Sky?"

Mary sat down on a bench. "Nothing happened."

"I don't understand."

"I'm not ready to talk about it." She patted the bench. "Sit with me, Artie."

Patience was a virtue, but it was not Artie's virtue. "What's the matter?"

"I couldn't do it." That was all Mary would say about the events at Red Sky. "I couldn't do it."

"What couldn't you do?"

When he didn't get an answer, Artie tried again. "What happened tonight at Red Sky?"

"Promise me, you won't think I'm a horrible person."

"I could never think that."

"My mother was asleep. No one else was around. I realized I would never have a better opportunity. I picked up one of her pillows and held it over her face."

Artie didn't say a word, didn't move a muscle.

"I stood there for the longest time, the pillow some six inches above her face. I knew what I had to do, but it was hard. Finally, I lowered the pillow, until it was barely resting against her skin. I told myself to press down, but I couldn't do it. I threw the pillow to the floor and ran out. I was so glad to see you there on the street."

Artie chose his words with care. He knew that a wrong word would crush her. "I can't imagine how hard this has been for you, waiting for your mother to die. And every night, no matter what, you sit with her. You are an amazing woman, a wonderful daughter. Few people would have the strength to show up night after night. You're not a horrible person. You had a moment of weakness, but you knew it was wrong, and you stopped."

"Artie Mehlman," she said, her voice suddenly getting louder, "you're a damn fool." She punched him on the arm as hard as she could. "A double damn fool." Then she tried to explain, her voice barely a whisper. "I'm not upset because I wanted my mother to die. I'm upset because I didn't have the courage to go through with it."

Artie sat there, on the bench in Breakwater harbor, stunned. Mary rushed ahead, knowing if she stopped she would never say the words.

"She doesn't know who she is any more. She doesn't know where she is. When she doesn't take her pain meds, she screams about the unbearable pain. But when the nurse tries to get her to take her pills, she screams that they're trying to poison her. One by one, her internal systems are shutting down. She should have been dead months ago. For all intents and purposes, she is dead. You've seen her. That's not a life. I'm her daughter. I should love her enough to help her do what she can't do for herself. I should love her enough to help her die."

## 54

FOR THE FIRST TIME SINCE ARTIE TOOK A ROOM AT THE boarding home, Mary wasn't in the kitchen, preparing breakfast. He peered up the stairs that led to her private third floor rooms, but nothing appeared to be out of the ordinary. There was nothing for Artie to do but sit in the parlor and wait for Mary to make an appearance.

Artie thought about Mary and her mother, and then found himself thinking about Johnny Gee and Johnny Gee Junior. He thought about the choices that people make and the ones they don't make. He'd been thinking a lot about making a life in Breakwater, Maine. Suddenly that seemed unlikely. Anyway, it was for the best. He was crazy to think a girl like Mary could fall for a guy like him.

It was after nine when Mary walked down the stairs, out the door and off to church, without so much as a good morning. Without a goodbye.

With Mary out of the house, Artie retreated to his bedroom. He had come to Breakwater with little in the way of material possessions. Other than the lobstering clothes, he had acquired nothing in Breakwater of any value. Nothing except Joe's lobster money. Artie felt bad about it, but he shoved the cash into his kit bag.

He pulled out a pen and paper. He stared at the blank paper and gave up. There were no words that would excuse what he planned to do. It would be better for Mary not to know. Artie grabbed his kit bag and left the boarding home, closing the door behind him. In the rearview mirror, he could see Edmund, standing on the porch, watching him drive off. One more secret for Edmund to add to his collection.

Artie drove past Red Sky without stopping. It was quiet on a Sunday morning. He drove around the block and parked on the street behind the convalescent hospital. He removed a small vial from the kit bag. In the weeks since he first arrived in Breakwater, he had nearly forgotten about the small vial.

There was a fire exit at the rear of the Red Sky Convalescent Hospital. He checked the door carefully. It didn't appear to be alarmed. Slowly, he opened the door and stepped into the stairwell. Another door opened onto the rear hallway. Artie waited until the hall was quiet. Then, as fast as he could manage, he went down the hall to Ida's room. He slipped inside. The door closed with the faintest of clicks.

Ida heard the click. She sat up in bed and spotted her visitor. "Are you here to take me to the dance?" When Artie didn't answer, she grew agitated. A nurse came running down the hall. Artie hid in Ida's closet, crouching behind her nightgowns. He could hear the nurse talking in soothing tones to her patient.

"I'm going to give you a shot, Ida. It will make you feel better."

Moments later, all was quiet in Ida's room. Artie slipped out of the closet. The nurse was gone. Ida was sedate, but her eyes were open, her voice a murmur. "Are you here to take me to the dance?"

"Yes, Ida. I'm taking you to the dance."

A weak smile formed on her face. "Thank you."

Artie took the vial from his pocket and poured a few drops of liquid onto his handkerchief. It would all be over in a few minutes.

The next few minutes were the longest minutes in his life. Artie expected someone to bust open the door and catch him in the act. But, a few minutes later, it was done. Ida had found peace. At least, Artie hoped it was peace he saw on her face. He put the handkerchief in his pocket and cracked the door open.

The hallway was deserted. He slipped out as quietly as he had come. Artie hurried to his car and drove off. He pointed the car south for the long drive home to New York.

Thirty minutes later, he pulled the car to the side of the road and took a deep breath. There was nothing to tie him to Ida's sudden death. He had a kit bag full of Joe's lobstering money. He could go anywhere. The question was, where did Artie Mehlman want to go?

Joe was sitting on the porch with Mary when Artie parked his car out front of the boarding home. He grabbed the kit bag and joined them on the porch.

"How was it?"

Artie stammered. It took him a minute to realize Joe was talking about the lobster catch. It seemed like an eternity since Joe had asked him to work the boat solo. He reached into his kit bag and handed Joe the cash. Without counting, Joe handed most of it back to Artie. "You earned it."

"Are you hungry?" Mary asked. There were two pizza boxes sitting on the porch. "I know it's not a proper Sunday dinner, but what would you say to a slice?"

She opened the first box. Joe grabbed a slice with peppers and onions. Artie was choosy when it came to pizza. "What's in the other box?"

The ring of the telephone interrupted her. Mary went into the kitchen to take the call. Artie opened the second box and selected a slice of pepperoni. It wasn't as good as the pies he used to get in Long Beach, but it wasn't bad. He could learn to like it.

Five minutes later, Mary rejoined them on the porch. "That was the nursing supervisor at Red Sky. My mother passed away."

Joe gave Mary a hug and offered his sympathies.

"I need to go to Red Sky. Can you drive me, Artie?"

"Of course."

Artie felt strange walking into Red Sky with Mary. The nursing supervisor, Miss Simpson, was waiting at the reception desk. She gave Mary a big hug.

"I'm so sorry for your loss."

"Thank you."

"Your mother is in a better place."

"I know. I'm trying to take comfort in that. What happened?"

"According to Dr. Wignall, her heart finally gave out. She died in her sleep."

"Where is she now?"

"She's still in her room. Dr. Wignall signed the death certificate. After you're done, we'll arrange transport to the funeral home. With your permission, of course."

"Thank you. I'd like that. Do you need me to sign anything?"

"We can do that later."

"If you don't mind, I think I'd find it easier to deal with the paperwork now."

"As you wish."

Miss Simpson pulled several papers out of a folder and started to explain what they were.

"It doesn't matter anymore." Mary took the papers and signed them.

Miss Simpson walked them down the hallway. She stopped outside Ida's room. "I'll leave you here. If you need anything, I'll be in my office."

"Thank you."

"Again, I am sorry for your loss."

Mary grabbed Artie's hand for support and walked into her mother's room. Ida was lying on a gurney, ready for transport.

Mary sat down, crying softly. She said her goodbyes to Ida.

"Do you think we can leave without talking to the staff? They mean well, but I don't think I can handle them right now."

"We can slip out the back door."

"There's a back door?"

"Follow me." Artie led her down the rear hallway to the fire exit. They exited through the stairwell and out onto the street in back of Red Sky.

They walked around the block, got in the car, and drove home. In the car, Mary and Artie talked.

"I need to go to the funeral home tomorrow. I need to make proper arrangements."

"You don't have to make any decisions right away. Give yourself time."

"I've had five months. How much more time do I really need? Later this week, maybe Wednesday or Thursday, I'd like to have a morning viewing, followed by the funeral service and burial. When we get home, I need to call the minister."

But when they got home, Mary didn't call the minister. She sat on the porch, lost in thought.

"Is there anything I can do?"

"I don't want to think about Ida." Mary had a faraway look in her eyes. "I want to think about her when she was still Claudia, when she was young and full of life."

"Tell me about Claudia."

She attempted a smile. "Claudia was a wonderful mother. She made every day a celebration of the present. And then, she got sick and it was my turn to take care of her. Whatever time she had left, I wanted it to be a celebration of the present. If it made her happy to be Ida, I was okay with that. But her sickness robbed her of the present. In the end, all she had were bits and pieces of a life."

Artie left Mary alone with her memories. He checked on her from time to time. Joe did the same. Even Edmund and Roy checked to make sure she was okay.

The third time Artie checked on her, Mary spoke up. "We need to talk."

Artie sat down on one of the Adirondack chairs.

"No," she said. "Not here. Come with me."

They walked up the stairs to the third floor. There were three rooms—Mary's bedroom, a sitting room and a third room— "My mother's room," Mary said.

Artie didn't know what he was supposed to do. He stood there, rocking from one foot to the other, waiting.

Mary went to the closet and pulled out an old cardboard box. "Here," she said, and handed the box to Artie.

Inside, Artie found bits and pieces of Mary's childhood . . . report cards, photo albums, Barbie dolls . . . news clippings.

He read the newspaper stories. When he was finished, Artie didn't know what to say.

"I was eight years old when my father raped me."

Mary recounted the story. She spoke without emotion as she told him the story of her eighth birthday and the court case that followed.

"We had ice cream cake and pony rides at the party. My favorite was Dobbin, a lively and handsome little pony. I spent most of the party riding Dobbin in circles around the house. When the party was over, I was tired and ready for bed. Daddy came into my bedroom, and I'll never forget what he said. He said, 'You're a big girl now and you deserve a big girl birthday present.'"

Mary didn't tell him exactly what her Daddy had given her. Anyway, Artie had read about it in the papers.

"Even then, I knew what my Daddy did was wrong, but he was my Daddy and I was his little girl. No, he explained proudly, I was his big girl. After the second time, I got into the habit of pushing my bureau in front of the door when I went to bed.

"And then, one day I got home from school and my father was gone. I didn't ask, and she didn't tell. Or maybe she didn't ask and I didn't tell. I'm not sure which. But somehow she knew. I think mothers always know. She told me my father had to go away. And then, a day came when I had to put Mom in the hospital. Going through her things, I found the cardboard box. I will forever be thankful that my mother was able to shield me from the ugliness of the court case and the inevitable small-town gossip."

Artie sat next to Mary on the sofa in her mother's bedroom, stunned and silent.

"When Mother got sick, I was determined to help her get better. But she didn't get better. She got sicker, and my choices got more complicated."

Mary pulled a photo album out of the box. She turned the pages slowly, pointing to Polaroids of Claudia. Claudia dancing. Playing tennis. Fishing. Mugging for the camera. Claudia, arm-in-arm with a handsome young man.

"Before I was born." Mary touched the photo. "Things would have been better for my mother if . . ." Mary didn't finish her thought. She wiped away a tear. "When I got home from church and you weren't here, I got worried."

"You don't need to worry about me."

"I've grown very fond of you, Artie Mehlman." Mary fiddled with the Polaroid. "When you're fond of someone, you worry about them."

He took Mary's hand. "There's nothing to worry about."

"What were you doing today while I was at church?"

"Nothing."

"Really? Nothing?"

"Nothing important."

"It was important enough that you packed up your room. I thought you were gone." She looked him straight in the eye. "Isn't there something you want to tell me?"

He couldn't meet Mary's gaze. "Nothing that you need to know."

"If you say so." Mary frowned. "I need to be alone now. I have some thinking to do."

She pushed Artie out the door and down the flight of stairs.

# 55

THE RUSSELL FUNERAL HOME HAD BEEN IN BUSINESS IN Breakwater since 1890. Jonathan was the third generation of Russell men to satisfy the town's funerary needs. He knew Mary. He knew her mother. He was fairly certain that he knew what her mother would have wanted. Mary's instructions took him by surprise.

"Are you sure that's what you want?"

Mary was adamant. "That's what I want."

"It's none of my business, but it feels like you're making a rash decision."

"I appreciate your concern, Jonathan. I want you to know this isn't the emotional decision of a grieving daughter. I prayed on this all night."

"I'll make the arrangements."

Red Sky notified the authorities about Ida's death. She was an elderly woman, diagnosed with Parkinson's, whose heart had finally given out. There was nothing that warranted an investigation, but even in the most benign of circumstances, there was paperwork that was required. At the Breakwater Police Department, Officer Hilliard drew the assignment. He made an appointment to meet with the nursing supervisor. There had been a time when a simple phone call would have been sufficient, but the rules were changing, even in Breakwater. He drove to Red Sky before closing the file on the dead woman.

Officer Hilliard had never been inside the convalescent hospital and wasn't sure what to expect. He stopped at the reception desk and signed the visitor's log. He spotted Mary Townsend's signature repeatedly as he scanned down the page. His meeting with the nursing supervisor was routine, two professionals dotting their i's and crossing their t's. There was nothing out of the ordinary about Claudia Townsend's death.

Nothing, that is, until Officer Hilliard got back to the station house and thought about the visitor log. Before taking any action, he called Red Sky and asked the receptionist to read him the names. He pulled a note from his desk and called Detective Miller of the Nassau County Police Department.

"Detective Miller here. What can I do for you?"

"This is Officer Hilliard, calling from Breakwater, Maine."

Detective Miller turned on the speakerphone, without even thinking about it.

Tommy listened carefully. Later, the detective would quiz him about the call. Detective Miller was grooming him to be a good cop. When the time came, he would be ready. But it felt to Tommy like there was more to it than that. Like he was supposed to be the son Miller never had. Only he had a son. Ben.

"Did you find Artie Mehlman?"

"Sunday night a woman died in a local hospital. She was an elderly woman, diagnosed with Parkinson's."

"What does this have to do with Mehlman?"

"I'm getting to that. But you must understand, this was an unremarkable death. There was nothing that warranted an investigation."

Miller looked at the stack of paper on his desk. "Go on, Officer."

"I drove to Red Sky before closing the file on the dead woman."

"I don't mean to rush you, Officer, but please, can you get to Mehlman?"

"The dead woman's daughter visited her regularly. When I checked the visitor's log, I spotted Mary's signature repeatedly as I scanned the page. For the last several weeks, a man accompanied her. I didn't recognize the name at first. Then I remembered our phone call. According to the signatures on the visitor's log, the man's name is Artie Mehlman."

"Holy shit! Junior's still in Breakwater. Are you sure the old lady died of natural causes? Did anyone do an autopsy?"

"Like I said, there is nothing suspicious about the old lady's passing."

Miller nearly jumped through the phone line. "Junior Gee makes it suspicious. Where is the body now?"

"At the funeral home."

"Listen carefully, Hilliard. Go to the funeral home. Take a look at the old lady's face. If you see any red marks, a rawness, almost like burns, around her mouth and nose, call me immediately."

"If I find any red marks, what do they mean?"

"They mean that Junior murdered the old lady."

Officer Hilliard hung up the phone. The idea of helping to solve a New York murder case had been exciting. He wasn't sure how he felt about the possibility that Breakwater might have its very own homicide. He didn't say anything to the sergeant.

It was late in the afternoon by the time Officer Hilliard went to the funeral home.

"I'm here about Mrs. Townsend. If it's not too much trouble, I'd like to see the body."

"I'm sorry, Officer, but that won't be possible."

"I don't understand."

"This morning, Mary instructed me to cremate her mother."

# 56

WHEN HE WAS FINISHED WITH OFFICER HILLIARD, DETEC-
tive Miller looked at Tommy. "If I have a chance to question
Junior, I know I can make the case against Bayard."

"When do we leave?"

"I'll talk to the Captain."

Detective Miller went home before the end of his shift, surprising
his wife with a dozen red roses.

She loved roses, especially on her birthday and Mother's Day,
but roses on an ordinary day, that couldn't be good. "You're home
early. Is everything okay?"

"Everything's fine. But I have to drive to Maine." He handed
her the roses.

"They're lovely." She clipped the ends, arranged them in a
vase, and placed them on the dining room table. "You can't go to
Maine! What about Ben's court date?"

"It'll be okay. Mr. Cavendish will handle everything."

"You should be there."

"Yes. I should be. But I can't. I'm a Nassau County Police Detective, and that comes with responsibilities."

"What's going on in Maine that is more important than your son?"

"Nothing is more important than Ben. Not in Maine or anywhere else. But I still have to do my job."

"I'm counting on you to be there tomorrow. I don't want to do it by myself."

"I know, dear. If you like, I'll call Mr. Cavendish before I go."

"What's going to happen in court tomorrow?"

"The DA will tell the judge that he's signed off on a plea deal. The judge will ask Mr. Cavendish if that's true. Mr. Cavendish will confirm the settlement. Ben will plead guilty. He'll pay a hundred dollar fine, and then it will all be over. You'll be out of court before lunch."

"You make it sound so simple."

"It is simple. Now where do we keep the suitcase?"

"Do you want something to eat before you get on the road?"

"How about a sandwich? Ham and cheese if we have any."

She made him a sandwich, and as long as she was at it, she made one for Ben as well.

"When will you be home?"

Ben drove with his mother to the old courthouse in Kew Gardens. Mr. Cavendish said to meet him there at ten. They pulled into the parking lot at eight-thirty. Ben spent the next ninety minutes meditating—*om santih santih santih*. His mother spent the time drinking bitter vending machine coffee.

She jumped at the sight of Mr. Cavendish, in his fine gray suit, carrying his brown leather briefcase. "You're late."

Mr. Cavendish checked his Omega Constellation. It was nine forty-five. "I'm sorry, Mrs. Miller."

They sat together while Mr. Cavendish reviewed his case notes. Everything had been worked out in advance with the district attorney. Mr. Cavendish clapped Ben on the shoulder. "Just follow my lead, son, and everything will be fine."

Ben's mother kissed him. "I don't understand why they won't let me sit with you," she said, and then she hurried off to find a seat.

Ben walked into court with Mr. Cavendish and took his spot at the defendant's table.

Events went much as Mr. Cavendish had explained them. The DA advised the judge that they'd reached a pre-trial settlement. Mr. Cavendish concurred. The judge asked Ben how he pled.

"Guilty, your honor."

"You seem like a nice young man, but there are times when a nice young man needs to be taught a lesson."

Ben figured he could put up with a lecture from the bench.

The judge took a quick look at the settlement agreement. "I'm not convinced that a hundred dollars is sufficient."

Out of the corner of his eye, Ben could see his mother fidgeting in her seat.

Mr. Cavendish was stunned. "But your honor, we came to an agreement with the district attorney!"

The judge chose to address Ben rather than his attorney. "Did Mr. Cavendish advise you that as the judge, I am not bound by the terms of the agreement? Did he advise you that if you pled guilty, I am permitted to ignore the agreement and administer justice as I deem appropriate?"

"He did, your Honor." He also told Ben that such things didn't happen except in the most extraordinary of circumstances.

"Well, I have had a parade of nice young men in my courtroom for the last two days, all of whom broke the law in various ways at this so-called Festival for Peace. I think it is time to send a message, and the message is one night in jail."

"That's not fair!"

The judge looked out across the courtroom. "Who said that?"

"I did," Ben's mother said, jumping to her feet.

"And you are?"

"Ben's mother."

There was no role in the court proceedings for mothers. "I'll ask you to sit down and remain quiet."

"My son is about to start his graduate work at Princeton. He doesn't have time for this foolishness."

The judge was apoplectic. "Foolishness? Ma'am, I must warn you. Motherhood notwithstanding, you are on the verge of contempt."

Ben's mother always had to have the last word. Even in court. Especially in court. "With all due respect, your honor, you brought it on yourself. I find your actions in the court to be contemptible!"

"That's it! Bailiff, remove this woman and lock her up until she is ready to apologize."

Ben watched in stunned silence as the bailiff dragged his mother out of the courtroom.

"Now, where were we?"

The DA asked, "Can we approach the bench?"

The judge waved the attorneys forward. "What is it?"

The DA spoke quietly. "As you said, your honor, you have seen a parade of similar cases these past two days. All of them were settled with a hundred dollar fine. With all due respect, jail, even for one night, would create the impression of a lack of fairness."

Ben could see anger spark in the judge's eyes. The DA must have seen it, too.

"I know it's not your intent to create such an impression."

"No, of course not." The judge paused, weighing the likely fall-out from his decision. "It's possible that I misspoke. Step back.

"Mr. Miller, I hereby sentence you to pay a fine of a hundred dollars. If you come before me again, you won't get off so easily. Court is adjourned."

"What about the defendant's mother?" asked Mr. Cavendish.

"She needs a little time to ponder the seriousness of her situation. I'll instruct the bailiff to bring her before me in one hour. If she apologizes, I'll release her."

Ben spent the hour meditating—*om santih santih santih.* He tried not to think about how his mother spent the hour.

But an hour later, she apologized, and they drove home.

"Are you okay, Mom?"

She was surprisingly upbeat, considering her ordeal.

"I'm fabulous," she said. "Didn't you think I was fabulous back there?"

"I don't understand."

"He was about to sentence you to one night in jail. I couldn't let that happen. So, I distracted him. More than that, I gave him another target for his anger. And now we get to go home together, neither one of us sitting in that horrid jail."

## 57

ABOUT THE SAME TIME THAT MRS. MILLER WAS BEING LED away to jail, Detective Miller was parking his car in front of the Breakwater, Maine police station, Tommy Callahan riding shotgun. The detective was anxious about Ben's court appearance. He checked his watch. Assuming everything had gone according to plan, they would be on their way home from court.

The station house in Breakwater was much smaller than the Fifth Precinct, with none of the hustle and bustle. As they walked up the front steps, Detective Miller took a moment to remind Tommy of the rules. "Keep your mouth closed and your eyes open."

Officer Hilliard was waiting for them.

"Welcome to Breakwater. I've been instructed to babysit you while you're here."

After the long car ride, Detective Miller had no patience for small town cops. "Is there a problem?"

"Not yet." Officer Hilliard grinned. "The Chief is worried you might upset the serenity in our little town. It's my job to make sure you don't. I hope you're okay with that."

"I'll be on my best behavior." Detective Miller turned his attention to Tommy. "You too!" Tommy was getting better at keeping his mouth shut. Better, but not perfect. "I'd probably do the same thing if I was in his position," he said.

"Anyway," Detective Miller continued, "what did you learn when you went to the funeral home? Did you see any red marks on the old lady's face?"

"I was two hours too late."

"I don't understand."

"Mary Townsend instructed the funeral home to cremate her mother."

*Have we driven all this way for nothing?* "I need to locate Mehlman. I'd like to start at the hospital, unless you have a better idea."

"I'm not a big-city detective like you, but I do know a little bit about police work. You see, Mary Townsend runs a boarding home in Breakwater. Apparently, Artie Mehlman rents a room from her."

"That's good work, Officer. Thanks. We can start there."

When they arrived at the boarding home, Officer Hilliard introduced Miller as "the detective from New York."

"I'm sorry to bother you at this difficult time, Miss Townsend," Detective Miller began. "I understand your mother passed away. I am sorry for your loss."

"Thank you. But you didn't drive all this way to make a sympathy call. What can I do for you?"

"I'm looking for the man you know as Artie Mehlman."

"Is he in some sort of trouble?"

"I just want to ask him a couple of questions."

Mary Townsend was nobody's fool. "You've come an awfully long way just to ask a few questions."

"I believe that Mr. Mehlman can help me solve an open homicide. If he can, it will be worth the long drive."

"And if he can't?"

"Then I still had the pleasure of meeting you and Officer Hilliard."

"Mr. Mehlman rents a room, but you already know that, or you wouldn't be here. Of course, he's not here right now. He's at work." Mary turned to Officer Hilliard, adding, "He works with Joe."

Officer Hilliard explained, "He's working on a lobster boat. We won't be able to talk to him until tonight."

Detective Miller had a hard time imagining Junior Gee working as a lobsterman. "If you don't mind, I'll need the names of the other men who rent rooms here."

Mary looked to Officer Hilliard for guidance.

"It's okay, Mary."

"There's Roy DuClos, Edmund Webster, and Joe, of course."

"We'd like to talk to them, if it's not too much trouble," the officer said.

"Edmund's the only one here right now. He's not much of a talker, but you're welcome to try."

Mary introduced them to Edmund. "I've got chores to do," she said. "Call me if you need me."

Detective Miller turned to Edmund and smiled. He began with a simple question to break the ice. "Have you lived here a long time?"

"Yes."

"So, you know Artie Mehlman?"

"Yes."

"Have you noticed anything peculiar about him?"

"Peculiar in what way?"

"I don't know. Does he act strange?"

"He's from New York. That's strange enough."

"I'm from New York."

Edmund smiled broadly. "Yeah. I thought so."

"That's a good one, Edmund. So, anyway, I understand that Mary's mother died on Sunday."

"I remember before she got sick. She was a good woman."

"I'm sure she was. Where were you on Sunday?"

"Here."

"Do you remember whether Artie Mehlman was also here on Sunday?"

"I think so. Yes."

"Which is it, Edmund? Is it, *I think so,* or is it, *yes?*"

"I spent the afternoon on the porch. If he left the house, I would have seen him."

"Thank you, Edmund. You've been a big help." Detective Miller turned to address Officer Hilliard. "I'd like to say goodbye to Miss Townsend."

They located Mary waiting in the kitchen. Officer Hilliard said goodbye for all of them.

"Thank you for your time, Mary. We'll be leaving now."

But Detective Miller was not quite finished. "If you don't mind answering one question. Isn't it unusual to have the body cremated so quickly?"

Mary didn't answer, and the detective didn't press the issue. When they got into Officer Hilliard's cruiser, he looked at the detective and frowned.

"That is exactly the sort of trouble the Chief is hoping to avoid."

# 58

DR. BAYARD ASKED KAREN TO MAKE ARRANGEMENTS FOR A car service to take him to LaGuardia Airport. It was expensive, but the trip was critical to his future at Hanover Chemical. It was important that he be at his best. He considered telling Karen to have the car pick her up as well, but he knew the company would not approve such an extravagance for a secretary. As it was, he'd expended a good bit of good will getting her permission to fly. The comptroller had suggested that Karen take the bus and meet him in DC.

The Eastern air shuttle flew from LaGuardia to Washington National. They got in line at LaGuardia, paid cash on the plane for their seats, and before long, they had landed in Virginia.

If he had been traveling by himself, Dr. Bayard would have taken a room at a hotel near the Pentagon, but he wanted to give Karen the full DC experience. After doing a good bit of research, Dr. Bayard reserved a room at the Calypso Hotel. The Calypso, located on Q Street NW, had for many years been a meeting place for the district's high society. The Calypso advertised a long list of famous tenants, including, in their day, F. Scott Fitzgerald and Thomas Edison. Dr. Bayard expected the room rate to be considerably higher, but when he called, they quoted him a very reasonable rate. He wanted to impress Karen. He knew how appreciative Karen could be.

The cabbie was surprised when Dr. Bayard announced their destination. "You sure that's the place?"

Dr. Bayard's chest swelled with pride. "To the Calypso, my good man."

Dr. Bayard expected to find the Calypso in a swanky city neighborhood. From the safety of the taxi, they passed through neighborhoods that were neither fancy nor clean. Karen leaned in close. Dr. Bayard put his arm around her. "That's the way it is sometimes in cities," he explained. "One block is only so-so, and just a block or two away the neighborhood is opulent." In case she didn't understand, he belabored the point. "Watch for the neighborhood to get nicer as we get closer to the Calypso."

The neighborhood did change as they got closer, but not in the manner Dr. Bayard was counting on. The Calypso was a twelve-story dump. The hotel lobby was filled with heroin addicts and hookers.

Karen took one look and announced, "We're not staying here. Not one night. Not one minute."

But the taxi had already pulled away, and with it their luggage. Dr. Bayard was carrying his briefcase and Karen had her purse. Everything else was speeding away in the trunk of the taxicab.

"There must be a pay phone in the lobby. Call a taxi. Call the police. Call anyone you want, but get me out of here!"

The trip was not working out the way Dr. Bayard had planned. He was angry with the hotel. He was angry with the cabbie. He was angry with Karen. He raised his arm as if to hit someone, and Karen was the only one available (other than the heroin addicts and the hookers).

"Stop yourself, Duncan! I mean it. Put your hand down!"

He struggled to regain his composure. "I'll go make a call. Do you have a dime?"

Karen rummaged through her purse, pulling out her spare change. "Here."

Dr. Bayard took the coins. "I'll be right back."

"Oh no, you don't. You're not leaving me alone."

She grabbed Dr. Bayard before he could go off in search of a telephone.

"Wait here," he said as he stepped into the phone booth. Karen refused to let go and squeezed in with him.

They remained in the phone booth after Dr. Bayard had made his call, stuffed in like two clowns in a clown car. Eventually one of the hookers knocked on the glass door and told them that their taxi had returned.

The cabbie was contrite. "I didn't mean to drive off with your luggage." He opened the trunk. "I don't think this place has a bellhop."

"We've changed our mind."

The cabbie closed the trunk. "That's a good idea. Where would you like me to take you?"

Karen jumped in the back seat. "Any place nice."

Twenty minutes later, the cabbie pulled to a stop in front of the Grenadier. Dr. Bayard peered out the window.

"Is that the White House?"

"Yes. I think you'll be more comfortable here than at that other place."

"Thank you." Karen whispered in Duncan's ear, making sure the cabbie could hear, "Give him a huge tip."

Dr. Bayard walked into the lobby of the Grenadier. The comptroller would never approve his expense report.

## 59

BACK AT THE BREAKWATER POLICE STATION, DETECTIVE Miller challenged Officer Hilliard to step up. "You need to open a murder investigation."

"Do I need to remind you that I have explicit instructions from the Chief? I'm not supposed to let you cause any trouble while you're visiting. I'm pretty sure he'd consider a murder investigation to be trouble . . . a heap of trouble."

"I'm just trying to serve the cause of justice. I'd like to think you are, too."

"Hey, wait a minute. Look, an old lady died. She'd been diagnosed with an incurable disease. It was never a matter of if, only when. When turned out to be Sunday. The doctor at Red Sky signed a death certificate. The daughter had the body cremated. Even if I believe that she was murdered, which by the way, I do not, there's nothing for me to investigate."

"Okay, explain one thing to me, and I'll stop asking questions about the old lady. What was Artie Mehlman doing at the hospital?"

"I don't know. You asked me to keep a lookout for Artie Mehlman. I found him. End of story. Unless there's something you haven't told me."

Miller leaned forward in his chair. "Artie Mehlman's real name is Johnny Gee Junior. Junior, as we call him, is a killer for hire. His father was a contract killer before him. Senior now resides in Clinton Correctional. I'm investigating a murder case in New York, and I'm pretty sure that Junior is the killer. But I need Junior's cooperation if I'm going to nail the sonofabitch who hired him."

Officer Hilliard scratched his head. "Maybe that's all true. But there's nothing you can say that will convince me Mary Townsend hired a hitman to murder her mother. That's simply not possible."

Mary Townsend seemed like a nice young lady, and she lived in this quiet little town. It was unlikely she could find a hitman in Breakwater, even if she wanted to. Still, Detective Miller trusted his instincts.

Officer Hilliard had a question of his own. "On the phone, you told me to look for red marks on the dead woman's face. What's that about?"

"In the case in New York, the woman died of heart failure. According to the medical examiner, the red marks on her face meant that chloroform was the murder weapon."

"There's still no evidence to suggest that Mary's mother was murdered. Do you really think Mary would hire a hitman and also rent him a room? That doesn't make sense. There has to be another explanation."

"Maybe there is. But an investigation is the only way to find out. She seems nice enough. But why else would she bring a killer to the hospital? And why would she cremate the body?"

"It does seem odd."

"So, will you open an investigation?"

"No. I can't do that. But I can buy you time so you can ask a few more embarrassing questions before the two of you leave Breakwater."

"Thank you, Officer Hilliard."

"So, what now?"

"I'd like to question Artie Mehlman before he has a chance to talk to Mary."

# 60

"WHEN I GET BACK, WE NEED TO MAKE A DECISION ABOUT this place."

Willow and Bug were alone in the ashram. The kitchen was still closed by order of the health department. The longer it remained closed, the less likely it would ever re-open.

Bug nodded his head. "I'll talk to Sativa tomorrow. Maybe he can do something."

Willow tried to stifle a laugh. "Sativa can't even get us a court date." The troubles at the ashram had put a strain on their relationship. Willow was heading off to DC to join the Women's Strike for Equality. "I wish you would come with me."

Bug snorted. "It's a women's thing."

"You know better than that. Equality's not a women's thing. It's a people thing."

"It's going to be thousands of women getting together to complain about men. Under the circumstances, I'd rather stay here."

Willow laughed so hard that green tea came out her nose. "I'm not going there to complain about men. I love men. I'm going there to demonstrate against a patriarchal system that treats women like we're second-class citizens."

"It's not that bad."

"You're not a woman. I do the same work as the male teachers, but I don't get paid the same. Is that fair?"

"You make a good living."

"That's not the point."

"Then what is the point?"

Willow was tired of arguing. "Come with me. Maybe you'll figure it out. Maybe we'll figure it out together."

"This is really important to you."

"Yes. It is."

"Okay."

"You'll go with me?"

Bug smiled weakly. "I'll go with you."

Willow jumped up and gave him a big kiss. "I want to get there in time for the encounter groups."

"That sounds like fun."

## 61

BY MIDAFTERNOON, DETECTIVE MILLER WAS SITTING IN the harbor in Officer Hilliard's patrol car, waiting for the lobster boats to come in.

Hilliard pointed to a lobster boat heading into the harbor. "That's the one."

Detective Miller waited until Junior tied down the dock lines before climbing out of the cruiser. Tommy, in the back seat of the cruiser, kept his mouth shut and his eyes open.

"You're a hard man to find, Junior."

Dressed in his yellow slicker and rubber overalls, he surely didn't look like a hitman. Hell, he barely looked like a lobsterman.

Artie jumped at the sound. "You startled me." He cleared his throat. "Anyway, I think you've mistaken me for someone else."

Detective Miller spotted a slight twitch at the corner of Artie's right eye.

Joe walked over to join the conversation. "This is my boat. Can I help you?"

"I'm here to speak with Johnny Gee Junior."

"I'm sorry, Detective. I don't know a Mr. Gee."

"What about you, Mr. Mehlman? I'm sure you must know Junior."

"Maybe I do. Maybe I don't. Who wants to know?"

Detective Miller stared at Junior. "I drove all the way from Long Island, and I don't have time for games. I spoke to the guy at the tattoo parlor who supplied you with Artie Mehlman's identity. I spoke to the auto dealer in Connecticut who sold Mr. Mehlman a used car. So, let's cut the crap, Junior. I need to ask you a few questions."

Joe looked at Artie. He seemed concerned, but not especially surprised. "Is everything okay?"

Artie nodded. "I need a few minutes alone with the detective."

Officer Hilliard stepped in. "It's okay, Joe. I'll help you offload." He turned to Tommy, still sitting in the rear of the cruiser. "Hey you, kid, you can help too."

Tommy took one look at the mass of angry lobsters, their claws twitching, their pincers clicking, and declined Officer Hilliard's invitation.

While Officer Hilliard helped Joe offload the lobsters, Detective Miller had an eagerly anticipated chat with Junior.

"I'm investigating the Bayard murder."

"Then you came all this way for nothing. I don't know what you're talking about."

"I think you do. Rosalie Bayard. You murdered her in her bed on . . ." He checked his notes. "Friday, May eighth."

"Sorry, Detective. You've got the wrong man."

"In the weeks leading up to her death, you made several calls to Hanover Chemical."

"Maybe I was looking for a job."

"Yeah, I think maybe you were. I think Dr. Bayard hired you to murder his wife. I intend to nail Bayard, and you're the one who's going to help me do that."

"Let's say, for the sake of argument, that you're correct. Why would I help you?"

"Let me make this simple. I already have you on one murder. Two, if you're not careful."

"I had nothing to do with the death of the old lady."

"What makes you think I'm talking about Mrs. Townsend?"

"I'm not stupid. What else would bring you all the way up here?"

"I think the girl hired you to kill her mother."

Artie stiffened. "Mary had nothing to do with it!"

"You will admit it's unusual for a girl to bring a hitman to visit her mother in the hospital." Detective Miller paused. "And then for the old woman to die."

"It's not what you think."

"Then explain it to me."

Artie studied his hands, picking at a scab. "If you want my help with Bayard, you will leave Mary alone."

"First you give me Bayard, and then we'll see about your landlady."

"Sorry, Detective. That's not good enough."

"In that case, you leave me no choice." Detective Miller straightened up. "Johnny Gee Junior, you are under arrest for the murder of Rosalie Bayard. You have the right to remain silent. Anything you say can be used against you . . ."

"Blah blah blah. I get it, Detective."

In the excitement over the arrest, Tommy forgot his instructions and called over to Officer Hilliard. "Detective Miller has just placed Johnny Gee Junior under arrest. We intend to return with our prisoner to the state of New York, where he will stand trial for the murder of Rosalie Bayard."

Detective Miller shut him up with one sharp eye.

"Please excuse my overanxious partner," he said to Officer Hilliard. "But he is correct. And now I'd appreciate the assistance of the Breakwater Police Department to provide Mr. Gee with a secure place to spend the night. If you can do that for me, I will take him off your hands first thing tomorrow morning."

Detective Miller put Junior in the back of the patrol car next to Tommy. "Keep an eye on him."

Officer Hilliard drove them to the police station. "What should I tell the Chief?"

The detective smiled. "Tell him I'm done making trouble. I'll be leaving with my prisoner first thing tomorrow morning. Then he can have his quiet little town back."

With Junior tucked in safely for the night, Officer Hilliard had one more question.

"What about you and your partner, Detective? Where are you going to spend the night?"

"Just point us in the direction of the nearest motel."

"Nonsense. You will spend the night at my house."

"I don't want to impose."

"The missus would never forgive me for such a lapse of manners. I'll call her so she has time to clean the guest room. Not that the room isn't spotless already." Officer Hilliard chuckled. "You know how women are."

Officer Hilliard lived in a large home overlooking the water. "It's been in my family for generations."

Detective Miller pointed to the platform built into the roofline. "What's that?"

"A widow's walk."

He had no idea what that meant, but it didn't sound good.

Officer Hilliard explained. "This house was originally built for my great-grandfather. He was a sea captain. When the captain was at sea, it was the custom for his wife to go up onto the widow's walk and watch for the return of her husband's ship. Sometimes ships returned. Sometimes they didn't. Hence, the name."

"I see."

"Let's go inside. I want to introduce you to my wife and kids."

Officer Hilliard's wife, Nan, was a pretty little woman. They had a boy, five years old, and a daughter, three, Henry and Rebecca. Becky curtsied. Henry shook the detective's hand and then Tommy's.

Detective Miller complimented the boy on his firm grip. Henry blushed. His father beamed.

"Would you like a drink, Detective?"

"Thank you. And please call me Stanley."

"I'm Tad." He poured three brandies, but Tommy politely declined.

"I can't drink that stuff."

Nan offered Tommy a cola.

There were family photos throughout the house. The detective's eye was drawn to one in particular—Tad, no more than eighteen years old, in uniform, covered in mud.

He waited until dinner was over before asking. "Did you see action in Vietnam?"

"I spent thirteen months in Pleiku. What about you, Detective?"

"WW2. Casablanca. Rome. Munich."

"Do you have any children?"

"A son, Ben. He just finished college."

"If you don't mind my asking, is he entering the service?"

"No. Ben will start grad school next week."

"Good for him. If there's one thing I've learned, it's that Vietnam is no place for children."

"I used to think we had a responsibility to defend South Vietnam from the Communists." Detective Miller struggled to find hard words. "Now, I'm not so sure." A tear formed in the corner of his eye. "Ben's older brother Billy was killed in Da Nang."

# 62

DUNCAN BAYARD AND KAREN CONAWAY AWOKE IN THE splendor of a Grenadier king suite. Karen rolled around in the oversized bed. Dr. Bayard was getting ready for his meeting at the Pentagon.

"Come back to bed," Karen purred.

Dr. Bayard was half-dressed, sitting at the desk, reviewing his presentation. His pants hung in the closet. Karen knew all too well what that meant. He didn't plan to put his pants on until he was ready to walk out the door. He wanted everything to be perfect for the Pentagon, even the crease in his trousers. Dr. Bayard was confident that the chemists at the Pentagon would be impressed by his lab results. He didn't want anything to shake his confidence. Not his trousers. And definitely not Karen.

"I don't have time."

"Not even for a quickie?" Karen crawled out of bed and under the desk, eager to show Duncan what she had in mind.

"I mean it, Karen. Not now."

Karen climbed back into bed and turned on the television. Duncan put his notes in the briefcase and finished getting dressed.

"Wish me luck."

"You'll be fine, Duncan. Your presentation is perfect. I should know. I typed it."

"Thanks for your help." He stood at the edge of the bed and gave her a kiss. "What are you going to do while I'm at the Pentagon?"

"First, I'll call the concierge and ask him to send me up a bellhop. When I'm done with the bellhop, I might go on a tour of the White House."

Dr. Bayard chuckled, but when he left for the Pentagon, that's exactly what she did. Service at the Grenadier was exceptional.

Dr. Bayard took a taxi to the Pentagon. He expected at least one chemist along with a couple of high-ranking Pentagon officials, perhaps even the Under Secretary. Instead he was greeted by a civilian procurement officer, who thanked him for coming and took him inside to a cubicle. The procurement officer didn't bother introducing himself. A tag on his shirt identified him as Kelly.

"I understand you have a new chemical agent you want to tell us about."

"Will anyone else be joining us?"

"One of my colleagues might be able to sit in, but anyway, let's you and I get started."

Dr. Bayard began with a brief explanation of deforestation. He skipped the more technical chemistry and focused on the key concept, that Hanover Chemical had developed a new product that would kill trees and vegetation, making it easier for American troops to track Viet Cong movement.

"That's very interesting. You do know that we already have a contract for such a chemical agent?"

"Yes, of course. But I am confident you will find that we have developed a superior product."

"I'm sure you have," Kelly responded, his voice flat. "But I spoke with our experts yesterday, and they are quite satisfied with our existing deforestation activities."

Nothing about the trip to Washington was going the way Dr. Bayard had expected. "With all due respect, Mr. Kelly, the chemical industry is a close-knit community. I would not be doing you a favor if I didn't tell you what the scuttlebutt is among chemists. We've heard about problems with your chemical agent. We've heard that it's not as safe for human beings as you would like to believe."

"I appreciate your candor, Dr. Bayard, so let me be candid as well. If what you say is true, and I have seen no evidence that it is, do you really think we're concerned about health risks to the Viet Cong? That seems more like value-added from where I sit."

"I can see why you might think that. But surely you want to protect the health of the American boys who track the Viet Cong through the jungle."

"Philosophically, the Pentagon couldn't agree with you more. But as a practical matter . . . Anyway, on behalf of the Department of Defense, I'd like to thank you for coming in today. I'll send your report to our experts. If they have any questions, I'll be in touch."

Dr. Bayard saw three years of research crumbling in a Pentagon cubicle. "When should I expect to hear from you?"

"As I said, if our experts have any questions, I'll be in touch." Mr. Kelly stood up and shook Dr. Bayard's hand. "Let me show you the way out."

# 63

BEFORE KAREN COULD REACH THE WHITE HOUSE, SHE found her path blocked by a crowd, mostly women, mostly in blue jeans, many carrying signs. One woman carried a sign that said, *It's Time for a Female President.* A long-haired man held up a sign that said, *You Don't Have to Be Female to Be a Feminist!*

She poked one of the women and asked, "What is all this?"

The woman was dressed in bell bottoms and a tie-dyed T-shirt, wearing sandals and carrying a book by Betty Friedan. The young woman beamed. "We're on strike!"

"What sort of work do you do?"

"Don't you get it? Women's work! We're on strike until we get the respect we deserve."

Karen wasn't dressed to protest. She wasn't sure whether she belonged. "Can I join you?"

"Groovy." The woman handed her a sign. *Equal Pay for Equal Work!*

Someone shouted, "There's a march on Connecticut Avenue," and the crowd moved off, Karen among them, determined to march for equality.

After the march, Karen joined up with a couple dozen women who had formed an encounter group of sorts. Standing in a circle, the women told their stories to a supportive chorus of *Sister!* and *Right On!*

The first few women told essentially the same story. Nurses who wanted to be doctors. Housewives who wanted to be engineers. When it was Karen's turn, she was ready to share her story.

"I am here today by accident. I didn't know about the Women's Strike for Equality, but I'm glad to be here. I have had plenty of experience with inequality."

Women in the circle cheered her on. It felt good to be part of the sisterhood, to be among people who listened.

"I'm a secretary. I'm here on a business trip with my boss."

At the mention of her boss, several women in the circle booed.

"He's not only my boss. He's my boyfriend."

That brought a louder round of boos.

"We've been dating for a couple of years. Not dating, exactly, he's married. Well, anyway, he was married. He told me he loved me, said he wanted to be with me, and promised me he would get a divorce."

A woman in the crowd yelled, "You don't need him!"

Karen shook her head. "The thing is, I do need him. And not just for the job. I'm not as strong as the rest of you. He's a bit of a jerk, but I love him. Two months ago, his wife died. I thought we would finally have a chance to be together, but I realize now I've been fooling myself."

Karen decided that the Women's Strike was more fun than a tour of the White House. She was proud of herself for speaking up. She made herself a promise to try to be stronger. When she got back to the hotel, she was surprised to find Dr. Bayard in the hotel room, their suitcases packed.

"How was your meeting?"

"I don't want to talk about it."

"Well, I had a fabulous day. Did you know that today is the fiftieth anniversary of the woman's right to vote?" Karen peeked at the suitcases. "Where are we going for dinner?"

"We're going home."

The lessons of the Women's Strike were fresh in Karen's head. "I'm staying here, in Washington, until tomorrow, the way we planned."

Dr. Bayard was grim. "We're not here on holiday. This is a business trip and the business is over. If you stay, you can't expect Hanover to foot the bill. Me either, for that matter."

Women's equality was slipping away. "When do I need to be ready?"

Dr. Bayard checked his watch. "The car service will be here in an hour." He gave her a kiss and tossed her on the bed.

For the first time in weeks, he was able to finish.

## 64

THERE WAS SOMETHING ABOUT THE WOMAN TELLING HER story to strangers on the street that Willow found touching. When she mentioned the death of her boss's wife, Willow nearly fainted. She had seen the woman once before, at Emily's home after Rosalie Bayard's funeral.

Willow slipped away from the circle of women and went in search of Bug.

Equality for women might not be as important to Bug as civil rights, or ending the war, or achieving enlightenment, but in its own small way, he decided, it was probably a good thing. Protesting anything was a good thing. Besides, it was important to Willow and that was reason enough. He hooked up with a group of like-minded men and wandered off toward DuPont Circle.

Willow found him at a sidewalk bar, drinking beer, deep in conversation with three feminists, all of them feminists with a Y chromosome, two of them in patched jeans with hair down to their shoulders, one dressed in a business suit. He jumped up when he saw Willow approach.

"You were right! Let me introduce you to the guys. Those two are Kevin and Dave," he said, pointing to the hippies, "and the well-dressed brother, that's Speedball."

Bug had spent the day talking to men who described themselves as feminists. By comparison, he recognized he was falling short. "When we get home, what do you say we get rid of the kitchen and convert the ashram into a women's center?"

Willow laughed. It was just like Bug to jump right in. "What will we do at the women's center?"

"I don't know." He shrugged. "Women's stuff."

Willow gave him a kiss. "I love you."

"I love you, too." Bug grinned. "It doesn't matter what we do, as long as we do it."

## 65

"I WANT TO FILE A COMPLAINT AGAINST THE DETECTIVE," Junior said as soon as he arrived at the Fifth Precinct.

The Captain was waiting for them. He ignored Junior's announcement and greeted the detective warmly. "Nice work, Miller."

"Thanks, Cap."

"You too, Tommy." The Captain grinned. "Did he give you any trouble?"

Tommy looked to Detective Miller for guidance. Was he supposed to answer the Captain's question, or was this some kind of test? Miller nodded.

"He flapped his gums all the way from Maine. And here I thought he would exercise his right to remain silent."

Junior tried again to gain the Captain's attention. "Hello. Can anybody hear me? I said I want to file a complaint against the detective."

"Tommy, would you do me a favor and take Junior's complaint? Then put him in a cell."

"Will do." Tommy took Junior by the arm and led him to an empty desk in the squad room. He pulled a pad of yellow paper out of the top drawer. "What's got your panties in a bunch?"

"We just spent twelve hours in the car."

"So what?"

"So, the whole time, that detective made me sit with my hands cuffed behind my back. Do you have any idea how much that hurts after twelve hours?"

"I'm not the one who told you to hide all the way up in Maine. Next time, find a hiding place closer to home. I hear Elmont is nice this time of year."

"You're not going to take my complaint, are you?"

"Of course I am." Tommy showed him the page filled with notes. "Here in the Fifth, we take pride in serving our citizens, even the scumbag murderous ones."

Tommy could hear the detectives laughing. It sounded good, almost like he was one of them after all. "Now that I've taken your complaint, I'm going to put you in a cell."

When he was finished, Tommy went in search of Detective Miller. The detective was speaking with the Captain.

"Like I said, that was a good bit of police work, bringing in Junior. What now?"

"It's been a long couple of days. I'm going to let Junior stew in the holding cell until morning. Tomorrow I'll see if I can get him to roll over on Bayard. And now, I'm going home to get some sleep."

"How's your wife?"

"What do you mean?"

"The stunt she pulled in court. Everybody's talking about it."

"What did she do in court?"

The Captain suddenly grew quiet. "Don't you know?"

"I have no idea what you're talking about."

"Well, if your wife didn't tell you, I'm not going to be the one that spills the beans. Go home and get some rest." The Captain grinned. "Tell your wife we're all proud of her down here at the Fifth."

Detective Miller drove home, doing well above the posted speed limit, grateful he was a cop. He pulled into the driveway, let himself in the side door, dropped his suitcase, and grabbed a cold beer from the fridge. "I'm home," he shouted, fumbling through the utensil drawer. "Where's the opener?"

Mrs. Miller came running. "I'm so glad you're home." She rummaged around in the utensil drawer until she found the opener.

Detective Miller kissed his wife . . . not for the opener, well, not only for the opener. "Where's Ben? How was court?"

She blushed. "Everything happened just the way you said it would. I don't know why I was so worried."

"So, everything went according to plan?"

"Of course. The judge accepted the settlement. Ben paid the fine. We were home in time for lunch."

Detective Miller stared at his wife and then gave her another kiss. "That's my girl."

## 66

"HOW'D YOU SLEEP, JUNIOR?" DETECTIVE MILLER HOPED that a night in holding had made Junior more agreeable.

"Lousy."

"Sorry to hear that. I, on the other hand, slept like a baby. Like a baby dreaming of cracking a homicide."

"Keep dreaming."

"I don't get it. You were so pleasant in the car."

"It's the city, Detective. It makes me cranky." Junior shook his head and sighed. "You know, I don't think I'm a New Yorker anymore."

"What are you?"

"A Mainer."

"If this is your attempt at some cockamamie insanity defense, it won't work." Detective Miller led him out of the cell and put him in interrogation room number one. "Wait here."

"Where else would I go?"

Tommy watched through the one-way mirror. Junior leaned against the wall and cracked his knuckles. In the next room, Tommy could hear the sharp crack.

After a few minutes, Detective Miller stepped into the interrogation room. "So, here's how this is going to go. You killed Rosalie Bayard. Before you killed her, you had several conversations with

Dr. Bayard. You could go away for a very long time, or you can make a deal. Give me Bayard, and I'll talk to the DA about a reduced sentence."

"I told you two days ago what my cooperation would cost."

"The Townsend woman."

"You got the police in Maine all riled up. I need to know she's okay. I need your assurance they're not going to open a case against Mary. Until I know she's okay, you get nothing from me!"

"I don't dictate what gets investigated in Breakwater, Maine."

"Maybe not. But you're the one who put the idea in the officer's head. So, this is on you, Detective. I'm telling you directly, Mary Townsend didn't pay me to murder her mother."

"Why do you care about that girl, anyway? Are you sweet on her?"

"That's none of your business. But if you want my cooperation, you'll deliver my message to the cops in Breakwater. Until you bring me a guarantee, don't waste my time with your plea deal. And if you ask me any more about the old lady in Maine, I want immunity. From now on, I don't talk about anything without my attorney."

"Let me see what I can do."

"That's better."

Detective Miller motioned for Tommy in the one-way mirror. Tommy escorted Junior back to his cell and then joined Detective Miller for a phone call to Officer Hilliard at the Breakwater PD.

"Hey, Tad. It's Stanley."

"Where are you?"

"Nassau County. Fifth Precinct. I'm in the middle of questioning Junior."

"You mean Mehlman?"

Detective Miller chuckled. "Yeah, Mehlman. Anyway, that's why I'm calling. He's worried your chief is going to open a case against Mary Townsend. He thinks I got you all riled up."

"Well, you did that for sure. The Chief put a reprimand in my jacket for letting you cause so much trouble."

"Geez, I'm sorry. So, can I tell Junior no one in Breakwater intends to look into the old lady's death?"

"I'm not authorized to speak for the department, but no, between you and me and Mehlman, no one up here will pursue Mary Townsend. Do you really think she paid Mehlman to murder her mother?"

"I don't know. Junior swears she had nothing to do with it, and I'm starting to believe him."

"But he's going to serve time in New York for your murder?"

"He will. You have my word."

"Even if the Chief was inclined to open an investigation, the truth is, we have nothing to investigate."

"So, the case is closed?"

"The case is closed."

"And it's going to stay closed?"

"Yeah." Officer Hilliard paused. "Still, like you said, it's one helluva coincidence."

Detective Miller hung up the phone and sent two patrolmen to pick up Dr. Bayard. He touched base with the Captain before speaking to Junior. "Call your lawyer. You've got a deal."

## 67

IT WAS MIDAFTERNOON BY THE TIME WILLOW REACHED Emily on the phone. "Meet me at the ashram."

"I'll be right there. Is everything okay?"

"I'm not sure."

Emily hurried to the ashram. Bug had a spool of paper unrolled on the table. He was feverishly drawing diagrams and taking notes.

"What's all that?"

Willow hugged Emily tightly. "Bug wants to transform the ashram into a women's center."

"Cool."

"Yes, it is. But that's not why I called you. I need to tell you something."

"What's up?"

"Don't hate me for telling you."

"Now you're being silly."

Willow took a deep breath and blurted it out. "Your father is seeing a woman."

"Mom's death hit him hard." Maybe he wasn't spending all his time at the lab. Emily sat down cross-legged on a prayer cushion. "He would never do that to Mom."

"I'm sorry, but it's true. Your father has been sleeping with his secretary for years."

Emily didn't want to believe it. "They just went away on a business trip."

"I know."

Since her mother's death, Emily had struggled with the emptiness in the house. But this went beyond emptiness. This was betrayal. She wanted to confront her father. She wanted to run away and hide. She wanted her mother.

Emily drove home and rummaged through her mother's stuff. Going through her closets only made Emily angrier. She located the Christmas card list. Even as Karen Conaway was sleeping with Emily's father, her mother had been sending the woman a Christmas card. Emily copied down the address.

# 68

DETECTIVE MILLER WAS IN THE SQUAD ROOM, READING the sports section and arguing baseball with Detective Johnson when the officers returned with Dr. Bayard.

"What do you want us to do with him?"

"Put him in room two."

Dr. Bayard was quieter this time. "I'm not saying anything until my attorney gets here."

It took a bit of effort to get all the players in their positions, but within the hour, Junior Gee and his attorney were in interrogation room one, and Dr. Bayard and the patent lawyer, Mr. Davenport, were in two.

Detective Johnson looked at Miller. "It's your case. Which one do you want?"

"Why don't you start with Junior? I'll take Bayard."

Johnson grabbed a folder and sauntered into room one. Detective Miller watched through the one-way mirror. "Gentlemen," Johnson said, nodding to the two men across the table, "you got everything you asked for. Now it's your turn. I'm going to sit back and listen while you tell me about the death of Rosalie Bayard."

With a nod from the attorney, that is exactly what Junior did.

"A mutual acquaintance introduced me to Dr. Bayard. He was looking for someone to dispose of his wife. Our friend suggested I might be able to help. The first time I called him at Hanover, we discussed Dr. Bayard's particular needs and preferences. It was Bayard who suggested the chloroform. He wanted it to look like a burglary. I pointed out it would be more convincing if the both of them were chloroformed."

"He was okay with that?"

"He was nervous, but he knew I was right. Seeing as how he was a chemist, he did all the calculations to make sure she died and he didn't.

"I called him a couple of days later and quoted him a price. It seemed to me that he was having second thoughts. So, I told him I needed payment in advance. I asked for five thousand dollars. He agreed, but I could tell he was getting cold feet. I called Hanover one more time to make arrangements to pick up the cash."

"How'd that go?"

"Bayard was in a meeting. Like I said, I thought he might back out, but it turned out I was wrong. His secretary told me he'd left a package for me. I drove to Hanover. The secretary met me in the parking lot and gave me the package. Five large."

Detective Miller had heard enough. The time had come to break Duncan Bayard. The detective entered interrogation room two, where Dr. Bayard was pacing.

"Detective Johnson has been talking to Junior," Miller said. "I'm sure you have a pretty good idea what they're talking about." He let that sink in. "Are you a gambling man, Dr. Bayard?"

"What do you mean?"

"Are you prepared to bet your freedom on whether or not Junior will keep his mouth shut?"

Miller watched Dr. Bayard. Then he turned his attention to the attorney. "While we're in here wasting each other's time,

Junior's in room one, spilling his guts. What do you think, Mr. Davenport? Do you have any words of advice for your client?"

"I want to point out one more time, for the record, that I am a patent attorney. I have advised Dr. Bayard that he should retain the services of a criminal lawyer, but he insists he's not a criminal. That said, my advice to all my clients is to tell the truth, the whole truth, and nothing but the truth."

"What's it going to be, Bayard?"

"I'm innocent."

"Sure, you are. Meantime, Junior's in there yapping it up. Three phone calls to Hanover Chemical. When he confirms the substance of those phone calls, we'll have more than enough to get a conviction, with or without your confession."

Now he had Bayard's full attention. Dr. Bayard sat up in the chair, rubbing his eyes. "Did you say three phone calls?"

"Yeah."

"I only spoke to him twice."

"What do you mean?"

"I mean there were only two phone calls."

"I'm listening."

"We talked about ways to resolve my marital problems. I explored the possibility of hiring Mr. Gee to do the job. But I chickened out. I realized I was still in love with my wife. Maybe I didn't like her enough, but I did love her. I couldn't kill Rosalie. I never reached an agreement with Junior. I never paid him a penny."

"Junior Gee doesn't kill unless someone is paying the bill. If it wasn't you, then who? Who else wanted your wife dead, enough to pay Junior five large?"

"I don't know, Detective." Dr. Bayard put his head in his hands, sobbing softly.

# 69

THE IDEA OF DR. BAYARD AND THE WAITRESS GNAWED AT Ben, refusing to let go. Ben couldn't explain exactly what he hoped to accomplish, but he had taken to hanging out at the Sunrise Diner, like he was returning again and again to the scene of the crime. Only it wasn't a crime scene, just a run-of-the-mill diner, and in any event, he never did see Dr. Bayard there. Ben didn't sit in Trixie's station, but she knew he was there. She approached him and said hello. "Off duty?" she asked.

Ben didn't know how to answer. "Huh?"

"You're out of uniform," Trixie said, by way of an explanation, "I figured you must be off duty."

Ben nodded his head in agreement. "Yes," he said, "off duty."

Trixie smiled shyly and touched him lightly on the arm. "I need to get back to my tables."

Day after day, Ben returned to the diner, waiting for something to happen. He watched Trixie from a distance, but each time, when he got up to go, he left her a generous tip.

Ben had given up hope of learning anything useful, but after a week of tips, Trixie approached him one more time. He was alone in a booth. She towered over him.

"Listen, kid, you're cute, but you're not my type."

"Is that why you think I come to the diner?"

She sat down across from him and played footsie under the table. "You could do worse."

"I have a girlfriend."

"And I have a boyfriend." Trixie Pilson laughed. "But I've been known to hook up if the guy is cute enough."

Ben took a deep breath and exhaled slowly. "Was Duncan Bayard cute enough?"

"Are you still hung up about that?" She stood up and walked to the counter, where she fixed herself a cup of coffee. "Do you want a cup?"

"Yes, please," Ben said. "With milk and sugar."

She returned with two coffees. "I've told you everything I know about Duncan."

Ben stumbled over the words. "Let's go through it one more time."

Trixie took a deep breath and exhaled slowly. "He came into the diner one night. Said his wife had locked him out of the house. He was cute. I felt sorry for the guy." She paused to stir creamer in her coffee. "But when I found out his wife was dead, I put an end to it."

They sat there, staring at each other, sipping coffee.

"This is the last time I'm going to answer questions about Duncan Bayard. So, if you've got anything left to ask me, ask it now."

"I guess I'm done." Ben drained what was left of his coffee. "There. Now I'm really done. I won't be bothering you again." Ben left a few bucks on the table and made his way toward the exit. "What was his wife's name?"

"Huh?"

"When Duncan Bayard told you his wife had locked him out of the house, did she have a name?"

Trixie Pilson scrunched up her forehead to help her remember. A smile broke out on her face. Ben couldn't help noticing, when she smiled like that, she really was a looker.

"Karen."

## 70

EMILY PULLED UP TO THE CURB IN FRONT OF A WELL-groomed ranch house in Merrick. The front walk was lined with begonias. She rang the doorbell and counted to ten.

Karen Conaway swung the door open wide. She was still dressed in her work clothes. Karen recognized Emily immediately.

"You're Duncan's little girl. Emily, isn't it? What a delightful surprise. Please, come in."

She led Emily into the kitchen. The avocado appliances gleamed. "This is my favorite room in the house. Can I get you something? I just brewed a fresh pot of Maxwell House." Without waiting for an answer, Karen poured a cup. "How do you take it?"

"Skim milk and saccharin."

"Of course." Karen brought out the milk and sugar substitute. "What brings you here on a beautiful Friday afternoon?"

"I want you to stay away from my father!"

"But that's impossible. I work for your father."

"You know what I mean."

Karen adopted a pained expression. "I am very fond of your father."

"Stay away from him."

"I'm sure this must be hard for you. I imagine your mother was the person you confided in whenever something was troubling you."

"Don't you dare talk to me about my mother."

"I want you to know you can count on me. Maybe it's not the same as a mom, but it could be."

"You're crazy. You could never replace my mom."

"Would you like something with your coffee? A cruller, perhaps?"

Chills ran down Emily's spine. "If you ever mention my mother again, I'll . . ."

Karen reached into the kitchen cabinet. "You'll do what?" She turned around. In her left hand, she held a box of crullers. In her right, a gun.

"You're crazy!"

Karen smiled, but there was a flash of anger in her eyes. "Don't say that!"

There was a knock on the door. "Miss Conaway, this is Ben Miller. I'd like to talk with you."

"Keep quiet," Karen whispered, "and have a cruller." The gun was pointed at Emily's head.

Karen dunked a cruller in her coffee. "This is nice."

"You're nuts."

"When you get to be my age, you'll understand."

"But I do understand. You've been sleeping with my father, putting ideas in his head. Maybe he did hire the hitman, but you were the one who pulled the strings."

Karen slapped her sharply across the face. "You're right about one thing. Your father is a weak man. Too weak to hire the hitman. I had to be strong for both of us." She smiled. "For all three of us."

There was another knock on the door. "Miss Conaway?"

Karen turned her head toward the noise. Emily had only a moment to act. She grabbed the princess phone off the counter and smashed the back of Karen's scalp. Karen went down with a crash. Ben busted open the door.

Emily heard sirens getting close. Police cruisers roared to a stop in front of the house.

By the time the police came rushing in, Ben was standing over Karen, pinning her to the ground.

Detective Miller was first through the door. "Ben! Are you okay?"

Ben grinned. So did the detective. He turned his attention to the business at hand. "Karen Conaway," he said, surveying the scene in the kitchen, "you are under arrest for the murder of Rosalie Bayard." A uniformed officer lifted her off the floor, cuffed her, and read her her rights.

Detective Miller checked on Emily. He smiled warmly, and for the first time in a long time, he wasn't being a detective. He was her boyfriend's father, and he was worried about her. "Are you okay?"

Emily smiled. "That felt good."

# 71

BEN COULDN'T SLEEP. NEITHER COULD HIS PARENTS. THE sun had just begun to peek out over the horizon, but his mother was already sitting at the kitchen table drinking coffee. His father was nowhere to be seen.

"Are you ready?" she asked when she saw Ben.

It was a big day, the day he was leaving for grad school. It felt like forever since commencement at Richardson.

"I guess so. I just have to pack Dad's car."

"You'll have to wait until he gets home."

"Is everything okay?"

Things had been crazy at the Fifth Precinct since the arrest of Karen Conaway. But the Captain had given Detective Miller the entire weekend off.

"Everything's fine, Ben. Better than fine. Your father will be home soon. Do you want breakfast?"

Ben wolfed down a bowl of cereal. "Can I borrow your car?"

"Where are you going?"

Ben didn't answer. His mother smiled. There was something different about the smile.

"I have to remember that you're not a kid anymore. I shouldn't be asking you what you're up to all the time."

"Thanks, Mom. I won't be long." Ben grabbed the keys, gave her a kiss, and ran out the door.

"Tell Emily I said hello."

When he rang the doorbell, Emily's Aunt Debbie opened the door and smiled warmly. "Come on in. I hoped we'd have a chance to say goodbye."

"Good morning, Mrs. Bayard. Is Emily home?"

"Of course. She's expecting you. And please, call me Aunt Debbie."

Emily came bounding down the stairs, throwing her arms around Ben.

Aunt Debbie cleared her throat. "I think what we're doing in Vietnam is wrong. I'm glad you spoke up at graduation."

Her comment took Ben by surprise. "Thank you, Mrs. Bayard."

She smiled. "Don't you mean, 'Thank you, Aunt Debbie'?"

It was Ben's turn to smile. "Thank you, Aunt Debbie."

"Anyway, I'll leave you kids alone. I'll be inside if you need anything."

"That's okay," Emily said. "We're going to the cemetery. I need to talk to Mom."

In the car on the way to the cemetery, Ben screwed up his courage and asked Emily about her father. "How are things between your Dad and you?"

"We had a long talk last night."

"When your mom died . . . he must have suspected the secretary."

"He was confused, depressed, and remember, it wasn't just Mom who'd been chloroformed. He was still recovering. But he's cooperating with the police."

"I guess that's a start."

They drove the rest of the way in silence. Ben parked the car in the cemetery lot. Emily made no move to get out of the car.

"He loved her."

Ben was pretty sure Emily was referring to her mother, but he decided to keep his mouth shut.

"I guess that sounds strange, after all that he did, but he told me he never stopped loving Mom." Emily took a deep breath. "And I believe him."

"And I believe you."

They sat for a moment lost in thought. Ben reached across the seat and took Emily's hand. "It's time."

Rosalie's grave was marked with a temporary marker. The dirt had settled and the grass was yellow-brown. Emily said a few words, *sotto voce*, a tribute to her late mother, a Catholic prayer, or possibly Hindu.

It was a short drive from Holy Redeemer to Beth David. Ben had promised Billy he would visit more often, but he hadn't gone back all summer. Ben couldn't leave for grad school without saying goodbye.

They parked in the front lot and took their time walking through the cemetery toward Billy's grave. They were fifty feet away when Ben spotted his father standing in front of Billy's headstone. It was too great a distance to hear anything, but it was obvious that he was talking to Billy.

Ben waited for his father to finish. Detective Miller smiled when he saw Ben and Emily.

He gave Emily a hug. "I'm sorry," he said, "sorry for everything."

There was so much Ben wanted to tell Billy, but the words got all jumbled.

Emily squeezed his arm. "It doesn't matter. Billy knows how you feel."

"You're right." Billy did know. And for the first time all summer, it felt like his father also knew.

"I love you," Emily said.

She tilted her head up slightly and Ben gave her a kiss. The perfect height.

"I love you."

*Om santih santih santih.*

# Acknowledgements

DURING THE TIME THAT I WAS WRITING HIT OR MISS, I served as President of the New York Chapter of Mystery Writers of America. So, I've spent the last few years engaged in nearly continuous conversations about the craft and the business of mystery writing, about the nature of good storytelling and especially about point of view. I can't possibly thank all of the authors, editors, booksellers, Board members and readers who took part in those conversations. Their thoughtful comments about what makes for a good story informed my decision-making as I wrestled this story onto the page.

I knew when I started writing *Hit or Miss* that it was a different sort of story from my previous books and that it would need a different sort of publisher. I want to thank the team at WiDo Publishing for partnering with me to bring *Hit or Miss* to the marketplace.

And, of course, I cannot leave this page without acknowledging the support of my wife, Carol. I could say a lot more about Carol, and I probably will, but I'll say it tonight, quietly, over a plate of smoked salmon and a glass of Haut Medoc.

# About the Author

JEFF MARKOWITZ IS THE AUTHOR OF FIVE MYSTERIES, including three books in the Cassie O'Malley Mystery series and two standalone mysteries. Jeff was fifty when he wrote his first mystery, *Who Is Killing Doah's Deer*. Published in 2004, it introduced readers to tabloid reporter and amateur sleuth Cassie O'Malley. Cassie returned in 2006 in *A Minor Case of Murder* and again in 2009 in *It's Beginning to Look a Lot like Murder*. In 2015, his standalone black comedy *Death and White Diamonds* won a Lovey Award and a David Award.

After graduating from Princeton University, Jeff spent more than forty years creating community-based programs and services for children and adults with autism,  including twenty-five years as President and Executive Director of the Life Skills Resource Center, before retiring in 2018 to devote more time to writing. Jeff is Past President of the New York Chapter of Mystery Writers of America.

Jeff lives in Monmouth Junction, NJ with his wife Carol and two cats, Virgil and Aeneas.